I0618307

A FLAWED JEWEL

A FLAWED JEWEL

A MARSDEN ROMANCE BOOK ONE

DAWN BROWER

MONARCHAL GLENN PRESS

This is a work of fiction. Names, characters, places, and incidents are products of the author's imagination or are used fictitiously and are not to be construed as real. Any resemblance to actual locales, organizations, or persons, living or dead, is entirely coincidental.

A Flawed Jewel Copyright © 2015 Dawn Brower

Cover art by Victoria Miller

All rights reserved. No part of this book may be used or reproduced electronically or in print without written permission, except in the case of brief quotations embodied in reviews.

"Love looks not with the eyes, but with the mind,

And therefore is winged Cupid painted blind."

— **WILLIAM SHAKESPEARE**

CONTENTS

My stepsister, Amanda, encouraged me to write a book, and in less than a day I had a really rough draft, in less than a week a short story ready for submission. If she hadn't goaded me into it, this book wouldn't exist. Thanks to Melanie for reading my really rough first draft —I know it was a mess of epic proportions in the beginning, to Hailey for her words of wisdom and showing me my many errors in a humorous light, and finally to Victoria for pointing out I was a little too bloodthirsty and for answering my endless questions. If not for all of your encouragement and help, I would have been lost. The three of you helped me more than words can express. Thank you for being my rock when all I want to do is hide under one. I love you girls.

Mostly I want to dedicate this book to my dad. He always believed I should write a book, but I never believed I had the patience for it. I wish he could have been here to see me finally getting around to doing it. I miss you daddy.

CHAPTER ONE

March 3, 1861

"You need to suck in more, Miss Pieretta."

Tully, her maid prodded and pulled at the strings of Pieretta's corset to tighten it as much as possible. One of many torturous things a lady must endure to remain fashionable. It was her job to get Pieretta ready for the biggest voyage of her life. There was nothing Pieretta wanted more than to stay on the plantation where she grew up, but her presence was required at her grandpere's estate in France. She had no real desire to go anywhere. Everything she knew was in Charleston. She had no choice but to go live in a country she knew nothing about.

Tully yanked on the laces one last time squeezing Pieretta's ribs tightly inside her chest. She struggled to breathe. Pieretta squirmed in an effort to loosen the stays. "Miss Pieretta, please, we need to tighten this corset a little more, or you will never fit into that traveling dress you had the seamstress make for you. We all know you're only stalling so you don't have to leave the plantation. Your grandpere is expecting you, and you need to be on that ship."

"Oh be quiet, Tully. The laces are too tight. Fix them before I can no longer breathe." Stupid know-it-all maid thought she could order her around. It was bad enough that her entire life was about to change. Now she had to deal with Tully ordering her around. "The dress will fit and still allow air to enter my lungs. Mind your own business and do as you're told," Pieretta scolded her.

As a southern belle, she didn't have to do anything more than host parties and help her father manage the house. The most traveling she had ever done was to attend picnics and soirees at neighboring plantations. She had never traveled more than fifteen miles away from her home. The idea of sailing all the way to France—Pia hated to admit it, but it terrified her.

Pieretta had never boarded a ship, now she was expected to sale on a long voyage. She, at least, had seen one or two while they were in the Charleston harbor, but it had never crossed her mind ever to give one a closer look. It was not an experience she ever expected to have.

Her happiest moments were in Charleston, in the heart of the only home she had ever known.

Pieretta didn't want to leave everything behind. It was hard to comprehend why her grandpere insisted she come live with him in France. The fact she didn't have any living male relatives in Charleston shouldn't matter. She could look after the plantation and deal with the overseer. Her father made sure she understood every aspect of running the plantation. She had the best education possible. He believed females had a right to learn more than just how to run a household or proper etiquette.

Oh, Papa, I miss you so much...

A sting of pain hit her chest. She was reminded again of her father's death a month ago. Each day without her father was more unbearable than the one before it. Pieretta couldn't believe she had to live in a world where he no longer existed. His death had been so sudden—had suddenly just quit breathing. It had been so devastating to realize someone could die without any warning.

Pieretta was all alone in the world.

She had no brothers or sisters, and her only

living relative was her grandpere. So it was with a heavy heart that she prepared to make the journey to live with him in France.

Her mother died when Pieretta was born, and her father never remarried. He loved her mother too much to ever envision a life with someone else. The only females Pieretta spent time around on a regular basis were servants. Without the benefit of a maternal influence, Pieretta had more masculine ideas about her future. It would have been all right to stay and run the plantation if she had been a man, but as a woman, she had no real say in her life until she reached her majority.

Until then, her grandpere, Comte Renard Dubois, had the right to tell her how to live her life.

Because she had never been to France, she didn't know what to expect once she arrived. Grandpere had told her stories about his estate and how large it was, but she had never had the opportunity to visit. He outlined the many gardens and the different foliage that it encased. Pieretta looked forward to walking amongst the roses and counting the various shades his gardener cultivated.

She had never seen an actual rose, but her grand-pere's description made them sound like the most beautiful flower on Earth. The blossoms were rumored to be filled with an aromatic scent that tantalized the nose. Rose buds bloomed in a variety of colors from the shade of a blushing bride's cheeks to the various hues of sunshine bouncing through the windows of her sitting room. Even with the allure of seeing roses for the first time, she still had no desire to travel such a long distance.

All of her trunks were packed and already aboard the ship. The only thing required of her now was to get herself ready, get in the carriage, and travel to the docks.

Pieretta wanted to throw a fit and stomp her feet, but that would be out of character for her. While her father often indulged her, Pieretta was not prone to temper tantrums. She did occasionally let her displeasure be known, but most of the time she was able to hold back the temptation to scream. Pieretta took a deep breath and exhaled slowly, preparing herself for whatever the journey might entail.

She stood up straight as Tully finished tying the corset's laces. She didn't want to stand still any longer than necessary and keeping still ensured the bows on her dress were tied evenly.

In her mind, fighting the inevitable would not help her situation. The servants needed to make sure she made it on the ship. Even though Pieretta didn't to move to France, she could make the best of the situation. Her life on the plantation had a repetitive quality to it—nothing ever changed.

Instead of harping on the negative, she could look at this forced trip as an adventure.

"Almost done, Miss Pieretta."

"It's taking forever," she groaned. Sometimes being female was a nuisance. Surely it didn't take this long for a man to get dressed.

"It'll be all done before you know it and then we will be boarding a ship to France."

Did Tully have to give her a reminder of it?

Tully finished lacing her stays, and the corset hugged every curve of her torso. She walked over and picked up Pieretta's traveling gown and opened it for Pieretta to step into. Once she was fully within the confines of the dress, Tully pulled it up and began the long process of latching all of the hooks up the side. She opted not to wear any petticoats or a hoop skirt, as it would be ridiculous to wear them in the small confines of the ship. Her traveling costume was made of the finest dyed black wool.

Black Wool was ever so dull and boring, but Pia didn't mind wearing it to honor her father. She'd miss him for the rest of her days. When she received the letter from her grandpere, Pieretta visited her favorite seamstress to have a few traveling costumes made for her crossing to France. She had no idea what the current fashion was and figured more gowns could be made upon her arrival at her grand-pere's estate.

Besides only so much could be done to make a black gown look good...

She was trying to be practical, and Grandpere wouldn't mind. He would want his little princess to be happy. After all, one couldn't be happy if one wasn't fashionable. Grandpere believed she didn't have the brains for anything besides frivolous things such as fashion. He did not realize Pieretta had a lot of things on her mind, and fashion wasn't always at the forefront.

Soon he'd realize how mistaken he was about her character.

For instance, her love of mythology consumed her. Some of her favorite books housed stories of the gods and how they had fallen. She read everything from Norse to Greek mythology. Her favorite had always been Thor. Pieretta often wished she could visit Asgard and have the opportunity to meet him and Loki.

"Tully, please tell me you remembered to pack my favorite books."

"Yes, ma'am" Tully nodded. "You have more books packed than you do gowns."

"Books are more important."

"hmmph" Tully snorted. "I wouldn't know as I've never had the opportunity to learn to read."

"Maybe I will teach you on our voyage. Not like we have anything better to occupy our time with."

"I don't know how much use I'd have for learning." Tully frowned. "Why don't we just wait and see how the crossing goes. You might find something to entertain yourself with."

Pieretta sighed. No one truly understood her—especially her only living relative.

Grandpere knew next to nothing about what Pieretta actually liked. He assumed she was similar to her mother, Dominique Dubois Carlyle, who only thought of frivolous things such as the latest styles and idle gossip.

Her grandpere couldn't be more wrong.

He usually visited her at least twice a year, staying for a few weeks and then returning home. Her mother was his original princess. Grandpere had doted on her his whole life. When her mother died, he had been heartbroken. When he saw his new granddaughter with her mother's royal blue eyes and pale blond hair, he had decided that he had a new princess to coddle with affection. It had helped to ease the sting of his loss, finding a near carbon copy of his beloved daughter. He'd found a way to fill the empty hole in his heart with Pieretta.

Tully finished connecting all of the hooks on Pieretta's dress. She inspected her work, trailing her fingers over the dress to smooth the lines. Stepping away, Tully motioned for Pieretta to sit down on the chair next to her vanity. "Miss Pieretta, you need to sit down so I can fix your hair."

She had no idea what Tully meant by fix her hair. She hadn't touched it. "What are you going to do to my hair, Tully?" Pieretta asked.

"Don't you worry any, Miss Pieretta. I am just going to pull it back a bit so it's out of your way. You're not going to want to deal with it on that there ship. It needs to be more manageable."

Pieretta sighed and sat in front of her vanity. Unfortunately, she had to deal with Tully even though she was a meddlesome nuisance. Tully had helped raise her, the servant believed she had a right to dictate how Pieretta should live her life. Tully's many lectures were a normal part of her day. In Pieretta's mind, Tully was overstepping her duties and trying to take the place of the mother she never knew. The maid was traveling with her only because a young unmarried lady could not travel alone. She was going to be the only person Pieretta would bring with her into this new life.

"I suppose you're right," Pieretta agreed. "It would be rather tiresome to constantly push my hair out of the way."

"Trust me, I know what I'm talking about."

Pieretta rolled her eyes. "Oh? And exactly how many ships have you sailed on?"

"I haven't always been on this plantation," Tully informed her. "I came over here on a ship when I was a tiny thing. Of course, my hair didn't have the opportunity to get blown around, but I do remember the howling winds."

"Howling winds?" Pieretta gulped. "What do you mean?"

"There was a nasty bit of storm for half the journey. The winds whipped right through the ship leaving an eerie whistling piercing our ears."

That didn't sound—appealing.

Tully pulled Pieretta's braid tighter and wrapped it around her head. Pieretta sighed, fighting tears as Tully continued to plait her hair. It was difficult to keep her emotions from welling up and spilling out of her. If she had one wish, it would be to find a way out of the situation her grandpere had forced her into. Her only option wasn't really an option in her mind. She could get married, but she didn't want any person to have that sort of power over her life. Relinquishing control meant fighting for the right to make any decisions for herself. Marriage was the one thing Pieretta had never wanted.

When she turned twenty-five, she would gain control of the plantation. It would be a long seven years living with her grandpere, but if anyone could do it, she could. Pieretta had to make sure her grandpere knew she was never going to get married. In Pieretta's mind, any woman had the capability to make her own decisions. It would be a cold day in hell before she allowed a man to have any kind of control over her life or her inheritance. Her father had made sure she was educated far beyond her station, and she had a working knowledge. She was intelligent and intended to use everything she learned to further her ambitions.

Tully finished fussing with her hair. Her pale blond locks were now securely wound around her head in a practical plait. Pieretta brushed a tear from the corner of her eye. Would she ever be happy again? She had serious doubts that happiness lay in her future. Pieretta stood and flattened her dress, smoothing the lines and wrinkles along the side of her skirt so it fell evenly as she moved. She glanced in the mirror. The dress wasn't designed to be flattering, but Pieretta believed she could make anything look good. She may be pale and sad, but she was still beautiful. She was curvy in all the right places with a small waist.

"All right, Tully, I guess now is as good a time as any," Pieretta said. "Go and have the carriage brought around. I'm ready for an adventure. That's how I'm choosing to see this change in my life."

Eerie winds and all...

Pieretta stood and looked around her bedroom one last time. Several years would pass before she could return and take control of the plantation. It was important that she store all of the good memories so the years in France would be easier to bear.

The fight to gain control over her life would be tough, but the things that mattered the most were worth fighting for. Even though at times she felt like she would never be happy again, Pieretta had hoped that she would find a reason to smile. Changes were always hard to make.

She wandered over to her bedroom door and pulled it open. She began the long trek down the stairs to the main hallway. At the bottom of the steps, she looked up as Tully made her way down the long staircase. No one ever promised life would be easy, and if Pieretta knew one thing, it was that she could get through any hurdle life put in her way. This was only one bump on a very long road ahead of her, but in the end, she knew she would get what she wanted. After all, Pieretta always did.

THE DOCKS WERE NOT a pleasant place to walk. They were filthy and smelled of unimaginable things. The scent of rotten fish and fresh salt water permeated the air. Pieretta needed to board the ship as quickly as possible, before she stepped in something disgusting.

The waterfront was booming with activity, and the noise was deafening. It was hard to ascertain the different sounds and locate where they might be coming from. The combination of the odors stung her nose and throat. The smoky air made her eyes water. Pieretta covered her nose with her hand in an effort to block out the stench but was forced to wipe the tears from her eyes as they started to stream down her face. Tully followed behind her as fast as she could. They both wanted off the docks as fast as they could manage it.

"Miss Pieretta, we need to move faster. I don't like it on these docks. Some of those men are making me uneasy. They're looking at us like we're a special treat they want to lap up."

"Don't be ridiculous Tully, they wouldn't dare harm us. We'll be fine. Just the same, there's our ship. Let's board quickly and be done with this area."

A lump formed in her throat. She gulped it down and refrained from looking at the men Tully referred to. They made her just as uneasy, but she refused to admit it.

They moved quickly to the gangplank so they could board the clipper. The ship had three large masts each filled to the top with five sails. When they stepped on deck, the first mate and captain greeted them.

The captain folded one of his hands behind his back with the other one tucked in front just below his chest and bowed to Pieretta. "It's a pleasure to have you aboard, Miss Carlyle. I am Captain Devere, and this is my first mate, Cam. I know Comte Dubois is anxiously awaiting your arrival in France."

"Do you know my grandpere well then?"

"As this is one of his ships, I have had many occasions to spend time with him, discussing how his shipments are to be handled. You are one of our most important cargos. He made sure to have a meeting with me before I left France and gave me the strictest instructions regarding your safety on this crossing."

Did he? She shouldn't be surprised, and yet she was.

"Grandpere can be very protective. I'm surprised he didn't make the trip himself."

"He wanted to, but an emergency arose at the last minute on one of his estates. It was something that required his personal attention. It is why he gave me instructions as to your passage and care. I hope your crossing with us is pleasant."

Pleasant? As far as she was concerned, there really wasn't anything that could make this journey tolerable let alone pleasurable. It took every ounce of her will to not come back with a rude comment. The need to get to her cabin and rest was starting to become a top priority to Pieretta. She needed to vacate the captain's company with as much haste as possible.

With as much politeness as she could muster, she cleared her throat. "I certainly wouldn't want it to be unpleasant. Who is to show us to our cabin?"

"My first mate will gladly give you a brief tour of the ship and show you to your cabin. We would prefer you remain in your quarters for most of the trip. It is the safest option. We will have a tray brought to you for all of your meals."

Was the captain mad? How could he expect me to be confined to a small room for three weeks? She would have to make her needs known from the very beginning or be stifled inside of a cabin with Tully for the lengthy passage. Her throat closed up just at the thought of it—she hated being confined.

"I couldn't possibly stay locked inside a small room the entire journey, Captain. We are going to be on the ship for at least two weeks. I would go mad for sure. I must insist on daily walks above deck."

The captain studied her for several seconds before he nodded.

"Very well, but limit them to thirty minute intervals twice a day. Do not walk on deck once night falls for any reason. If I tell you to get below deck, you are not to argue. Just go. I wouldn't insist unless it was a matter of safety."

"I can agree to that."

"Very well, Cam will see you to your cabin now."

The first mate guided Tully and Pieretta below deck and escorted them to their accommodations. There wasn't a lot of free space aboard the ship. The captain gave his quarters to the two women for the trip. Pieretta wondered where the captain would stay during the crossing to France. It would be cramped for all those involved.

Pieretta sighed as she entered the cabin. The limited space didn't leave much room for her to share with her maid. The journey across the ocean stuck in such a tightly confined room with Tully constantly telling her what to do might drive her mad. Tully scrambled in behind her, scuffling her feet as she settled into the small room. If only Grandpere hadn't demanded she come live with him. Why must females be dependent on their male relations?

"Thank you, sir. I think we will be fine for now. How long until we set sail?"

"If all goes well, we should be on our way in an hour's time. Please remain here for the rest of the evening. It will be too dark to walk on deck, and it is easy to fall overboard when you can't see in front of you."

"I will heed your advice, sir. I have no desire to swim, or sink, any time soon." Pieretta shuddered.

As the first mate left the two women, Pieretta only had one thought. *It's going to be a very long and grueling excursion across the immense ocean.*

CHAPTER TWO

A WEEK LATER…

"Captain Thor, sir. The ship has been spotted. The one you've been waiting for," bosun Cornelus informed him.

Thor lounged in his bunk. It had been an uneventful few days aboard the Sea Rover. He had waited patiently for the vessel leaving the American shore to cross paths with him. It carried a package he was desperate to get his hands on. That particular parcel held extreme importance to him—for one reason and one reason only. He needed it in order to finally get even with his former partner Renny Dubois.

The bloody man had organized Thor's early departure from this world.

If he hadn't been quick, he would instead reside in his eternal resting place. The bullet Renny had put into his shoulder would have entered his heart if he had not seen the glint of the pistol out of the corner of his eye. Since then, he had been patiently waiting for the opportunity to enact his revenge. As far as Renny knew, Thor died on that fateful night. The comte certainly hadn't bothered to check before he exited the docks as fast as his pudgy legs could carry him.

Thor had been twenty-four when his father died. At that time he inherited his father's business holdings along with the entailed property. Dubois-Marsden Shipping Firm was one of his more profitable business ventures. Thor had met with Comte Renard Dubois to learn more about the business side of the shipping company. He'd had a lot to learn before he could make sound business decisions. Renny took him under his wing and taught him everything. He trusted him completely. He'd been like a second father to him.

So it had come as a shock when Renny attempted to murder him. The brutal betrayal stung his pride and made it next to impossible to trust.

Thor had been on the docks in Paris overseeing the shipment of their latest cargo when everything changed. He'd looked up and saw Renny walking toward him. He turned to say something, and Renny pulled out a pistol, firing it at him. Thor had turned just enough preventing the bullet from hitting anything vital. His shoulder was nicked and he'd lost a lot of blood. With each wave of pain, he grew light-headed, causing him to lose his balance. His head had bounced off of the hard surface below him and knocked him unconscious. Renny, the bloody bastard, had left him for dead.

When he finally awoke, he had been surprised to find himself aboard a ship with his shoulder already doctored. Another captain had seen the whole thing and had Thor placed on his ship. It was on that ship, the Sea Rover, where he had made a life for himself.

It changed his life and from that moment on he became a new person, one that held no qualms about what must be done. Thor became an unscrupulous pirate—no bounty to small. Until the day would come when he'd become the Sea Rover's captain and his revenge became possible.

He worked his way up the ranks and, after a few years, he made first mate. When the old captain was killed in battle, Thor was promoted to captain as the laws of the ship dictated. He had been a pirate for five years now.

Snapping out of the distant memory, he looked up at his bosun with a smile on his lips. Thor had been planning his revenge against Renny Dubois for a very long time. All of his plans were finally going to become a reality. Today was going to be a very good day.

A cocky grin filled his face. "Corny, ol' man, that is the best news I've heard all day. Make the call, all hands on deck. We're about to plunder us a ship."

Soon he'd have his hands on the means to take down the most evil man he knew. It didn't matter that Thor had to sink to his level to obtain it. In his mind the means more than justified the end.

If Pieretta Carlyle let him he'd try to make it up to her later—hell even if she wouldn't he'd find a way.

PIERETTA WAS on the deck looking out at the ocean. She had taken well to sea travel and enjoyed having the wind blow on her face. If only she was allowed more than thirty minutes on deck each day to enjoy it, her life on board the ship would be more ideal. The waves danced and rolled across the ship's hull, crashing into it and creating white crested waves atop the cerulean horizon. She looked across the indigo waves and saw a ship in the distance. In fact it looked like it was moving toward their ship, growing closer with each gust of wind. As the other clipper's sails brought them closer to her, Pieretta squeezed the guardrail of the ship tightly. She bit her lip, the sting of her teeth drawing a minuscule droplet of blood. Surely they could see the two vessels were going to cross paths. There was a commotion to her left so she turned to see what was going on.

"Captain! Captain!" the first mate called out.

She looked over as the first mate ran toward the captain. His face was flushed bright red from running across the windy deck. Once he arrived at his destination he stopped suddenly and with a high pitched voice delivered the imperative message to Captain Devere.

"Sir, there be a pirate ship drawing close. It's flying the red flag, we're about to be attacked."

"Hurry, all hands on deck. Make sure our important passenger gets below deck," he shouted as he ran off.

"Wait. What does it mean when it's waving a red flag?" Pieretta asked the first mate. By the way Captain Devere and his first mate acted, Pieretta knew it wasn't a good sign.

Her heart beat hard against her chest. Pirates? Surely they were mistaken.

"Don't you worry none about that, miss. Just get below deck like the captain said."

"No, I am not going below deck until you answer me."

The first mate kept shooing her, his hands waving wildly in front of her face. He made sure she turned around and started the trek back to her cabin. When she didn't move fast enough, he pushed lightly against her back in an attempt to get her to move faster. If Pieretta didn't start moving faster, it was very likely he would shove her all the way to her cabin. He clearly didn't have time to deal with the hysterics of a young girl. From the expression on his face, it was evident he was weighing his options. He kept lifting his eyebrows and looking back at the approaching ship. They continued their journey to Pieretta's cabin. The first mate needed to follow the captain's dictate to ensure her safe return to her cabin.

He turned back with a frown on his red face. "It means they're going to give no quarter." A tinge of fear colored each word he spoke.

The words didn't mean anything to Pieretta. The

term was foreign to her. "I don't understand. What does give no quarter mean?" she asked him.

"They're not going to leave any survivors. They will kill us all if we allow them to board our ship. Go below deck as you were told." He scurried away. He had followed Captain Devere's orders and delivered her to her cabin—why should he care if Pieretta stayed inside. It was up to her to make sure she remained safely inside.

Pieretta's heart beat faster as the blood drained from her face. It frightened her, knowing that if the pirates boarded the ship they'd murder everyone. Pieretta quickly went inside the cabin and slammed the door shut. It was the only place she felt truly safe, but with each breath she took, she felt less and less protected on board the craft. She had never been more helpless than in that moment, thinking she was going to die. *What should I do?*

When she calmed down enough to look at her surroundings, she was surprised to see Tully paid no attention to her. Tully was unfolding one of her dresses and laying it across a table to smooth out the wrinkles, a complete waste of time in Pieretta's opinion. It wasn't as if she was going to wear it anytime soon. They were confined to the cabin.

Pieretta hadn't even considered this possibility

when crossing the ocean. How could she have? She had lived a very sheltered life. It occurred to her in that moment— she really didn't know anything. She didn't want to have regrets, and more importantly, she wanted to live. She had never been given the chance to do any of the things she wanted with her life. More importantly, she had plans—beginning with an expansion to the plantation and making the lives of the slaves better. Pieretta didn't believe in slavery, but she didn't have the authority to make any changes until she had gained her majority. There were so many books she hadn't gotten a chance to read, and so much she still wanted to learn. Damn those pirates for making her fear for her life.

"Tully, we are going to be attacked by pirates," Pieretta shouted, frustration flowing through each word she enunciated. "Put those away, we need to take cover."

"You be a silly girl, Miss Pieretta. We are not under attack by no pirates." Doubt was evident in Tully's voice. Instead of heeding Pieretta's advice, she turned her back and resumed her work.

Pieretta gasped. Why wasn't she taking her seriously? She stormed over to her side and shook her.

"Tully, I was just on the deck. I heard the first

mate and the captain. They are preparing for battle. Do not call me a silly girl!"

"Hmmph," Tully said, ignoring the warning. "Leave me be. I have work to finish." Tully turned around and resumed her task. Two seconds later she screamed when an earsplitting explosion hit the ship.

Pieretta jumped onto the bunk and covered her face in her skirts.

Tully joined Pieretta on their bunk, and they held on to each other. Tully squeezed her so tight it took everything Pieretta had to not push her away. They shook uncontrollably when another thunderous blast rattled the ship.

Pieretta closed her eyes, blocking out everything. She had never been a truly religious person, but in that moment, it wasn't hard to remember some of the prayers her pastor said during church services. The Lord's Prayer popped in her head, and she could hear the words loud and clear as if she was attending mass. With a shaky voice she began to recite them aloud, hoping if she died, the Lord would grant her some absolution.

THOR MADE his way onto the deck of the ship. With each movement his stride became more of a swagger. Most of the ship's crew were already tied up and secured in the empty cargo hold. His men were pretty savage when they worked, but they kept the casualties to an absolute minimum. A laugh rumbled through his chest, echoing across the deck. This vessel had been much easier to capture than Thor had anticipated.

It was a grand day to be a pirate.

The captain would be required to answer a few questions before they vacated the vessel. Thor walked over to where the captain was tied to the center mast of the ship, blood dripping from his mouth and a resentful look in his eyes.

"Well sir, I commend you on a fine battle," Thor said. "You didn't make it too easy. However, your job isn't quite done. You have something I want. Now, Devere, be a good sport and tell me where I can locate it."

The captain spit blood at him in response, hitting him square in the face. Thor wiped it from his eyes with the sleeve of his jacket. If the captain was looking to make Thor angry, he was doing a tremendous job so far. Captain Devere had better start cooperating before Thor would have to do something he disliked. He did not enjoy killing people and avoided it whenever possible, but the captain might just force his hand.

"Now, mate, that's not the way to go about this. If it's death you are looking for, I would be happy to oblige, after you tell me what I want to know. Where is Pieretta Carlyle? Tell me where she is, and I will consider letting you live."

The captain looked up at him through swollen eyes, now turning various shades of blue, black, and purple. "Why should I tell you anything? You are going to kill us anyway. I don't see the point of putting that girl through something that she doesn't deserve. I have no doubt that what you have in store for her is terrible. No one deserves to be tortured, even irritating females."

A cocky smile formed on his face. "Well that is no concern of yours."

The captain's face turned several shades of red at Thor's comment. "Go and bloody find her yourself." Each word uttered from his swollen lips was strained with barely contained rage.

"I know you work for that deplorable man Comte Dubois. I want to wring his neck more than yours. Don't be bloody stupid and save your own hide. Otherwise, I'll leave you for my men to torment. The choice is yours, mate. Now tell me where I can find her."

"You call him deplorable when you're a damned pirate. What makes you any better than him?"

Thor glanced at the captain's bloody and inflamed face, trying to decide how to best answer his question. He crossed his massive arms over his chest as he tilted his head up, looking at the billowing sails. After some careful internal deliberation, he chose the truth. "I keep my word."

The captain stared at Thor, disbelief clouding his eyes. His swollen lids folded down into tiny slits narrowing just enough to see the small specks of his black pupils shining through. "Why should I care about that?" he asked.

The man might just have a brain after all. He seemed to be considering his options.

"Well I guess that doesn't really matter, as your life is of little consequence to me. Whether or not you are still breathing depends on your willingness to help me locate Pieretta. Would you like to die now, or live to fight another day?"

Devere didn't take long to answer the question. He looked up at Thor. "She should be in my cabin with her negro maid. Good luck handling that one— she's a spitfire and stubborn as hell."

The Captain's head rolled back into unconsciousness. It bounced off the tall mast and landed hard against his left shoulder. The man would surely wake up sore if he remained in that position overly long. Thor couldn't muster enough energy to care and left him where he was.

Being a pirate was bloody business.

He stopped letting his principles get to him years ago. It was a hard life at sea every day, plundering ships for supplies. It went against his nature to kill, but if he was forced to, he never thought twice about delivering a fatal blow. Because he didn't believe in murdering someone without cause, he decided to leave the captain and his crew alive.

Thor wanted to make them suffer. He hated anyone working for Comte Dubois. Renny was rotten to the core. His precious granddaughter was the key to his undoing. Pieretta Carlyle would ensure his vengeance. Joy burst through his heart at the idea of finally making the comte pay. No words could express his delight.

He walked away from the captain's slumbering body to make his way below deck. He had a lady to locate so he could properly kidnap her. This was the fun part about being a pirate. A huge smile formed on his lips making his eyes crinkle at the corners.

Miss Carlyle would be the best prize he had ever plundered from a ship.

He couldn't wait to make her acquaintance.

The rest of the ship's occupants would be left tied up securely below the ship's deck, while the captain would remain tied to the ship's mast. It would depend on their will to survive if they managed to stay alive once the pirate ship left them to their own devises. If they were creative enough, one of them would come up with a way to free themselves and gain control of the ship. It would take some time for them to accomplish that task and would give Thor plenty of time to put some distance between them.

CHAPTER THREE

SHE PACED BACK AND FORTH FROM ONE END OF THE
cabin to the other. The quarters she shared with
Tully were small so she didn't have much room to do
it, but she couldn't stop herself. She twisted her
fingers together in frustration, debating what could
possibly be done. Pieretta stopped walking and
wiped her hands on her skirt to remove the damp-
ness building there. She continued her futile trek
between the two bare walls of the tiny room. The
cannons had stopped firing, and it was eerily quiet.
Tully had passed out from fear hours ago, rendering
her useless. Pieretta wondered if she should venture
out to see what had happened. She feared the ship's
crew was already dead. Pirates were surely all over
the ship by now.

A loud racket shook the walls of her cabin. She jumped when her door crashed open. The doorframe swallowed up by a man, his body filling almost every inch of the opening.

She swallowed the lump building inside of her parched throat. She had never been intimidated by a man before, but his demeanor was imposing. His whole body was nothing but muscle. He walked into the cabin and approached Pieretta. Once he was inside, she got an even better look at him. The more she saw of him, the more she wanted to escape. The pirate was perhaps the largest man Pieretta had ever laid eyes on.

And he seemed solely focused on her...

As the pirate moved around the cabin, she saw that black clothing covered every inch of his body. His pants were tight over his thighs. The man's shirt hung loose and flowed over his chest. It was open at the navel, revealing a small trail of hair. His immense stature towered over her small frame.

He was so—huge.

The pirate had to be at least six feet tall. His dark black hair was pulled back with a leather tie. A light dusting of stubble covered his face and added to his appeal. He was terrifyingly gorgeous. The pirate was the type of man that made you want to simultaneously run from and toward. He was by far the most handsome man she had ever seen.

How scary is it the only man I had ever been attracted to was a damn pirate?

Once he stepped into the light from her small lantern, she was able to get a better look at all of his features. His cobalt eyes narrowed into tiny slits with a purpose she could only guess.

Pieretta scrambled back towards the bunk in an attempt to get away from him. In her haste, she tripped over the dress Tully had been working on earlier and fell onto the bed face first. He stalked toward her and pulled her to her feet.

Pieretta looked up at him and saw a smirk forming at the corner of his mouth. One side was upturned in a lazy half smile. Her meager attempts at getting away were thwarted by the stupid dress Tully had carelessly left laying on the floor.

Even if I managed to get away from him where would I go?

They were on a ship in the middle of the ocean. She resigned herself to being at this pirate's mercy, at least for the time being.

"Ah, I have found a fine jewel to add to my treasure." He pulled her firmly into his tight embrace.

A musky smell tinged with a hint of sandalwood and chocolate filled her senses.

Delicious...

"What?" Pieretta dumbly replied.

How am I going to survive when looking at him makes me brainless?

"What is your name, girl?"

Should I tell him my name? Why does it matter to him what it is? Pieretta didn't know much about pirates, but the little she was aware of told her they didn't care about the people they attacked. Her name shouldn't matter to him. Still locked in his arms, Pieretta was forced to tilt her head back to stare up at him. The look in his eyes told her all she needed to know. It was best to just answer his questions and pray for mercy.

With great reluctance, she told him her name. "Pia."

"Ah, Pia, you're coming with me." He yanked her toward the door.

"No, I don't think so—I think I would rather stay here," she replied.

She really didn't want to go with the pirate. If she had the choice, she would rather stay on the ship and die with the rest of its inhabitants. Pirates were not known for their mercy or for treating prisoners well.

A female prisoner would suffer a fate worse than death.

Pieretta was horrified, and she did her best to fight her way out of his arms in an attempt to escape. She thrashed and pulled with all her might—only to have him laugh at her.

"The captain was right."

"About what?" She asked, stupidly. What else could she say?

"You're a feisty one. We're going to have a spot of fun." A cocky half smile filled his face. "Don't fight me. I promise you won't regret it."

Oh Lord. She started to pull again—harder this time. She had to do something—anything to escape.

Her efforts were futile as his grasp was so tight she could barely breathe. She squirmed in his arms with one last insufficient attempt to get away from him. She raised her small fists and pounded them with all of her might against his hard chest.

What is he going to do with me? I can't escape him. Where would I go?

Pieretta was at his mercy, on board a ship under his control in the middle of the ocean. She hadn't even told him her real name and had no idea why she did that. On further reflection, maybe she did know why. She had always hated her name, and Pia rolled off the tongue and sounded prettier than Pieretta. She decided right there from that moment on she would be Pia to everyone, including herself.

His amusement became evident as a rolling chuckle bubbled from between his full lips as he watched her struggle within the confines of his arms. It was the kind of laugh that rumbled through your soul. Once it started, Pia felt it all over her body, making her shiver with a need she didn't understand. She wanted to rub herself against him. Pia was suddenly aware of where she was. That little compulsion terrified her more than anything she had ever encountered. She needed to get away from him before she did something she would truly regret.

"Please don't take me with you," Pia begged again.

He stared down at her, disbelief clouding his eyes. "So you would rather die along with everyone else?" he asked her.

Pia felt the lump in her throat forming again. *He wouldn't kill me, would he?* Well if she was going to die, she would do her best to remain as brave as possible. There was no reason to give the man any enjoyment from her death. She wouldn't cry—would remain strong to the very end.

With a nod she said, "Yes, I think it would probably be better than whatever you have in store for me."

The pirate freed her long enough to grab her wrist and drag behind him. "Well it's good for you that I don't take orders, I give them. Come along, Pia. You're much more valuable to me alive than dead." He shook his head and frowned. "Lucky for you, my plans involve you still breathing, or I might have indulged your childish whims."

Good Lord, has the pirate captain claimed me as part of his treasure? If only there was some way to flee. She tried to pull away again, but he just laughed. Her attempt at escape had barely caused him to move an inch. Pia was doomed.

"You're a real bastard, aren't you?"

"I assure you, my father married my mother, and I'm legitimate." His amusement spread across his face as his lips curled into a smug smile.

Did he have to be so frustrating? He continued to chuckle at her attempts to pull out of his grasp. Pia had to restrain herself from using her free hand to slap him, for fear of what he might do to her if she gave in to the desire. He treated her like a bug that was easily ended with one stomp of his heavy boot. Perhaps the problem was the pirate could kill her without giving a second thought to what ending her life might mean. With her arm still firmly within his grasp, he continued to drag Pia along as they made their way topside.

"You know what I meant," Pia shouted.

"I don't read minds, and I don't assume to know what you mean."

Pia snorted. "How do people bear to be around your arrogance?"

"As long as they follow my orders, I don't care what they bear."

Her mind raced...the visual images almost made her fall over. What would this man look like bare? Pia had the sudden urge to fan her face with her free hand to alleviate the hot blush forming across her cheeks.

The sun hung low on the horizon, and she realized that she had been below deck for several hours. Tully had been passed out on the bunk for at least half of the—Wait a minute, what were they going to do with Tully? She should at least make an effort to save her. Tully had been her nurse since she was born. She may be bossy, but Pia would never wish her dead.

"I can't leave my maid. It isn't proper for me to travel alone."

"I could care less about your maid. My plans do

not include carrying around any extra baggage. Your companion will remain here in your cabin."

Pia was at a loss for words. She opened and closed her mouth several times before she was able to convey her shock at his causal dismissal. "You mean you're going to leave her here to die? That's deplorable. You're a wicked man, and I hate you."

The damned pirate ignored her as they continued their journey across the deck. He made his way to what could only be part of his crew. The group consisted of some men Pia had never seen before. She was familiar with most of the crew on the ship from her daily walks on deck, and she didn't recognize one person standing before her. That could only mean one thing; these were the pirates who attacked her grandpere's ship.

The pirate captain approached an older man with snow white hair and dark brown eyes. "Bosun Cornelius, take this treasure to our ship. Put her in a secure spot so I can deal with her later. Pia and I have much to discuss."

"Aye aye, Captain," he said, as he took over the captain's grip on Pia's arm. There were several red marks forming on her already sore wrist. The bosun yanked her across the plank connecting the ships.

Pia looked up at the sky and saw the red flag flying above her.

How can they live like this, taking the lives of the innocent? She could still see them plundering the ship, taking all the valuables. She wondered what they would do when they were done. The ship was badly damaged. Would they sink it?

"Where are you taking me?" Pia demanded.

The bosun acted like he didn't hear a word she said. Pia stomped her foot in frustration. She was strong and capable, and she would survive. The pirate could do his worst. She knew something he did not. She had a will stronger than most people, and she was a force to be reckoned with.

Cornelius marched her below deck, shoved her in a cabin, and then locked the door. Pia looked around the room. It appeared to be well kept. It was interesting to see the pirates were not slobs and took care of their belongings. The space was cramped, but it was not nearly as small as the cabin she had previously inhabited. The room held a large bunk and table. There was a trunk pushed up against the wall near the bed. Everything was bolted down to ensure it wouldn't move. The room was decorated in bland colors, everything a muted brown. Even the bedding was dark brown. As she finished surveying the room, she had a realization. Pia was in a room surrounded entirely by things the shades of dirt. Staring at everything in the place, it occurred to her she was probably in the pirate captain's cabin.

THOR SUPERVISED as the rest of the crew plundered all of the bounty the ship had to offer. The cargo from Comte Dubois's ship would bring in a good price. It was just another reason Thor was happy with the results from attacking the ship. That ship had been fully stocked with Dubois goods. There were crates full of rum, brandy, and several bolts of silk. It was a double win for him. He now had the comte's precious granddaughter and his cargo.

Thor had made sure every crew member had been breathing before they sailed away. Enough food remained in their galley to ensure they didn't starve. That is, if they managed to get themselves untied. He left the maid passed out in the cabin where he'd found Pia. If she was brave enough, she would free the crew members so they could continue their voyage to France.

Anything that could be used aboard the pirate ship had been taken. As a token of good will, Thor made sure his crew retrieved Pia's trunks. He wouldn't give any of them to her right away. He would make her earn the contents. He was going to enjoy every aspect of it too. Thor had already thought of several ways she could receive some of the things encased within her many trunks.

Thor walked on deck and sought out his bosun. He located Corny near the quarterdeck where he was issuing orders to some of the crew. "Make sure these cases of liquor are stored in the ship's cargo hold. Take the food to the galley and give it to cook. We will be eating well for the next couple of weeks." The crew members quickly marched off to move the cargo to the areas he had designated.

Corny turned at Thor's approach. "Captain, I was just making sure the bounty was secured," he said.

"Good. Corny, is everything where it needs to be?" he asked.

"Aye, Captain. We are ready to set sail as soon as you give the order."

"And my personal treasure?"

"She is in your cabin, as you ordered Captain."

"Very well, tell Jamieson to set sail. Those tasked with cargo organization can finish that as we sail. Have all hands on deck to open the sails and hoist the anchor. I will be in my cabin. I do not want to be disturbed unless it is a dire emergency."

"Aye aye, Captain."

Thor turned and made his way to his cabin. It was time to get better acquainted with his precious jewel. She truly was beautiful. The lovely woman only had one flaw, her irritating and evil grandpere. It wouldn't be long before Thor erased that flaw from existence. The only way to ensure the man paid for his crimes was to take away the one thing he valued more than money, his granddaughter.

CHAPTER FOUR

THE CABIN WALLS WERE BEGINNING TO CLOSE IN ON Pia, suffocating her with the knowledge that she had no clue what she ought to do. It had been several hours since the pirate's bosun had shoved her in the cabin, and she was slowly going insane. She was both uneasy and excited at the prospect of facing him again. Did he really murder everyone on board grandpere's ship? If so, why would he spare me and kill everyone else?

The pirate was a devastatingly handsome man, but his arrogance knew no bounds. Against her better judgment, she found herself attracted to him. Pia chewed on her bottom lip, concerned about what his plans were for her. She couldn't let that attraction be her undoing. She knew it was unnatural to feel the way she did, because he was clearly an evil man.

From what little she knew about him he didn't think twice about murder. Her body reacted to him of its own accord. Pia's heart beat faster and her face flushed with heat when she was near him. If she had met him in any other way, she would have seriously reconsidered her no marriage policy. He was the only man who had ever made her think it might be worthwhile to sell herself on the marriage mart.

Yeah, like a pirate would marry anyone. She snorted at the silly idea.

More likely he would plunder every inch of the woman's depths, leaving her well satisfied and alone for the rest of her life.

Well, now that's an idea.

She could not have those kinds of thoughts. She was a virgin and a lady. Women of her station did not consider gifting their virginity to pirates.

No matter how delectable they smelled or how utterly gorgeous they were.

He was immoral and diabolical, giving her the impression he was capable of almost any vice known to man. Pia couldn't help wondering why he took her aboard his ship. There was something he wasn't telling her, and her mission was to discover that reason. The first order of business would be to gain more information and ascertain why the pirate kidnapped her.

Pia roamed aimlessly around the room growing more frustrated at the lack of things to do. The room was stifling, and she was starting to feel claustrophobic from being confined for so long . She was not used to such idle musings and desperately needed something to occupy her time. Pia wished she had access to her trunks. She had lots of books, and it would be spectacular if she could get her hands on one of her treasured tomes.

It was very easy for her to get lost in books because she thirsted for knowledge. Her current book involved her favorite mythological characters: Thor, Loki, and Balder. Pia found Thor's hammer, Mjölnir, the most fascinating part of Norse mythology. It was rumored to be able to crush anything and could only be wielded by Thor himself. She could read about Thor for hours.

Pia desperately needed something to do and wished—again—she at least had some reading material to help pass the time. Even if there was some sewing, at least it would occupy her mind. Normally sewing would have caused her to want to poke her eyes out. Taking the sewing needle and blinding herself would have been preferable to sitting for hours and pulling it through some cloth. Sewing or cross-stitching was such sleep inducing work. In the meantime, she was bored out of her mind with absolutely nothing to occupy her time while she was locked inside the cabin.

She refused to give in to her frustrations or worry over something she had no control over. Surely there had to be a way to convince the pirate captain to release her unharmed. Her grandpere was wealthy—she was wealthy—between the two of them they could surely buy her way out of this predicament.

Yes, that was a plan she would broach with the pirate when he deemed her worthy of his presence, the rat bastard.

The sinfully attractive rat bastard.

She heard footsteps nearing the cabin door. Maybe that was the dreadful, gorgeous man now. Goodness gracious, she had to stop thinking of him in those terms.

How am I going to negotiate if I am constantly salivating over him?

He may be one of the best looking men she had ever encountered, but he was also the same man who ordered the attack on her grandpere's ship and killed its occupants. Well, except for her. Poor Tully, she didn't deserve to die. She irritated Pia, but she would never have wished her harmed in any way. The door creaked open, and the man himself walked in. He looked her over like she was his favorite dessert, and he couldn't wait to lick the plate, alleviating it of every inch of its sweetness.

Heat filled her chicks at his unadulterated gaze. Where was a fan when she needed one?

"Oh good, I can see you have been anxiously awaiting my attention," he drawled. Amusement laced through every syllable.

She opened and closed her mouth several times like a fish out of water trying desperately to breathe. Pia couldn't tell how many times, because she stood there dumbfounded at his audacity.

I should be terrified right? Pfft.

She had let go of that useless emotion hours ago. She didn't have time to be frightened anymore, and it wouldn't do her any good to give the pirate anything to use against her. It was high time she did something to make things go the way she needed them to. She would buy herself out of this situation with any means at her disposal. It was a good thing she was a very wealthy heiress, because it might just come in handy in this particular situation.

49

"I assure you, Captain Pirate, I have not been anxiously awaiting anything. What I have been is bored silly. If you were trying to kill me with ennui, then by all means stay the course. If not, well I will surely expire before long. Maybe that is your intention? It's less messy, and it's a great means of torture. It is a miracle I haven't already gone insane from sheer boredom over the past several hours."

A rich throaty laugh echoed through the room.

The man dared to laugh at her. It was like he couldn't help himself, and it just burst out of him every time she tried to speak to him. It was the kind of laugh that made you weary and excited at the same time.

When she first heard it, it made her shiver from the inside out.

She was starting to realize it might always have that affect on her. It tickled down her spine and made her tremble.

His laugh was dangerous.

Oh Lord. A devilish smirk curved his lips. She was a goner for sure. Damn man, why must you have such an appealing face. She was so lost in her own thoughts she almost didn't hear him when he finally spoke.

"Thor," he replied.

"Excuse me?"

"I am Captain Thor, not Captain Pirate."

It was Pia's turn to laugh. Only moments ago, she had pondered her favorite book on Norse mythology, and here the blasted pirate was named after her favorite hammer wielding god.

"I suppose you carry a hammer only you can lift right?"

"Oh, I don't have a hammer per se..."

She sucked in a breath as he delivered the innuendo. Pia choked, finding it difficult to express the words flowing through her mind. Surely he didn't mean what his words implied...

Thor's face lit up with his roguish smile, and he crossed the short distance between them and whispered in her ear. His hot breath caressed her neck as his words softly flowed through her eardrums. "I can assure you it will be my pleasure to share it with you."

Pia moved away quickly before she could take him up on his offer. Her heart beat faster. Its rhythm pounded through her ears and steadily gained pace with each breath she forced between her open lips. The more space she put between them the better off she would be. It was unfortunate the cabin was so tiny because it left her very few options. Pia needed to gain some distance between herself and the pirate. She took a deep breath and steadily exhaled with slow measures to gain some control over her body's reaction.

It was an attempt to remind herself she was supposed to be livid with him, not attracted to him.

Once her breathing was under control, she looked up into his blue eyes. "I am not interested in your over-inflated ego and images of grandeur."

Thor's lips upturned into a devilish half smile. There was once again a drop of mirth in each word he enunciated. "Oh, my ego is definitely not over inflated—or anything else. Trust me. It is well earned. However there is a part of me that is...inflated." He took a step toward her and asked, "Would you like me to show you?"

Thor's said the most outrageous things—Pia didn't know how to respond. Every sound and gesture he made was a form of seduction she was sorely unprepared for. Pia needed to steer the conversation on to another topic, one designed to ensure her virtue stayed intact. This one was taking her places she did not want to go—at least she didn't think she did.

Who was she kidding? A large part of her wanted to look him in the eyes and tell him exactly what she wanted him to show her. Her curiosity was going to get her into trouble.

What Pia needed to do was turn the conversation back on him. If she could make sure he didn't get any closer, she could remain relatively safe. "Pirate Thor?" she asked derision in her voice. "You imagine you are equal to a god?"

"I can't help what my parents named me, now can I?"

Disbelief coated her voice. "Your parents actually named you Thor?"

"Thor Williams, at your service," he said, making a production of bowing, much like a gentlemen would before a lady.

He seriously went by that moniker? His parents named him after a Norse god? No wonder the man had an overinflated ego. If he lived up to her fantasies about the god of thunder, then this Thor would certainly be her undoing.

Pia cleared her throat. "Sooo—I am Pia Carlyle. I don't know why you decided my life was worth keeping. Not that I'm not glad that you did, but I've had a lot of time in this room all by myself to consider my options. I thought maybe we could strike a bargain."

The man had a perpetual smile on his face, as if

everything she said was the most comical thing in the world. The real problem was his smile was so attractive she was having a hard time concentrating on her main purpose. If he kept doing that, she was going to climb all over him and beg him to show her his mythical hammer.

"Exactly what I came to discuss with you, Pia."

"Good. I am glad to see we are of the same mind."

He nodded. "I concur."

"I don't know if you are aware that my family has money. They will pay any ransom you demand."

"Oh, I am more than aware of who your family is, love," he replied.

"Good. So you will send notice of the ransom for my release?"

"I will do no such thing." He shook his head.

Pia's mouth hung open in frozen disbelief.

She recovered quickly while he continued to grin at her shocked disposition. In that moment, she realized this might not be something she could gain control over, but she still needed more information before she could assess what needed to be done.

"Why not?" she asked.

"I have other plans for you, dear. None of them involve extracting money from your grandpere."

Well that was a development she had not been

expecting. She assumed because he was a pirate he could be easily bought off with her inheritance. Her limited knowledge of pirates suggested they were mercenaries. From what Thor had said though this very well could be a personal endeavor of his, and her grandpere was deeply involved. "You know my grandpere?"

"I know him better than you do. In fact, he and I have a debt that will not be easily settled with the exchange of money. You are going to help me to do that, and in the process, we will get to know each other very well." He wiggled his eyebrow suggestively. "We'll be as close as two people can possibly be when this is all said and done."

With each sentence Thor uttered, Pia felt the color drain from her face. "What do you have planned for me?"

"You will find out soon enough. For now, we are going to get some rest, you and I. We have a long journey ahead of us. No need to rush into it right now. Our more pleasurable pursuits will happen in due time."

He dragged her toward his bunk. It was fairly large for a ship, but not nearly big enough for two people. Especially if he was one of those two people. It would definitely be a cramped sleeping space.

"Surely you don't expect me to sleep there with you."

"Oh, I assure you, not only do I expect it, but you will do it."

"It isn't big enough for both of us."

Thor smirked, and a small chuckle echoed throughout the cabin. He shoved her over to the side that hugged the ship. Pia curled up against the wall in an attempt to make herself as small as possible. She watched as Thor sat and removed his boots, setting them next to the bed. After the task was complete, he rolled over and lay next to Pia on the bunk. He pulled his arms over his head and tucked both of his hands beneath his dark locks. Pia tried to find a comfortable spot on the small bunk, but his body engulfed more than half of it.

"We fit just fine. You fretted unnecessarily, love. Don't worry, you will soon be very used to having my arms wrapped around you, in sleep and in other things. For now just lie down and get some rest."

"I'd rather not."

"Well that is too damn bad, lie down and go to sleep. You have no idea when you will have such a luxury again. I have many plans for you, and sleeping isn't exactly on my agenda."

Pia did what he asked, at least as much as she was

able. What else could she do? He was right in some ways. Pia would need some sleep if she was going to be able to properly deal with her dastardly pirate. She needed to survive, and Pirate Thor wasn't going to take advantage of her, much. She was still fully clothed at least. From what little he shared with her, she knew nothing was going to happen on this night, getting a little sleep would only benefit her.

Pia lay her head down on the bed next to Thor. Once she was curled up next to him, he rolled over and wrapped his entire body around her. She could feel his hammer nestled against her rear. If she gave him the slightest encouragement, she was sure he would show her what he could do with it. With what little preservation Pia still had within her, she ignored what that meant. She did not want to find out what losing her virginity felt like any time soon.

ONCE PIA WAS ASLEEP, Thor left the cabin and locked it. He couldn't stay in the bed with her any longer. She was too much of a temptation. He had plans, and using her body wasn't on the list.

Yet.

She called herself Pia. He liked it much better

than Pieretta. It rolled off of his tongue like a lover's caress, and they would be lovers. Every blush staining her cheeks told him how attracted she was to him. Her breathing became labored when he pulled her near, and he could feel her pulse racing beneath his fingers when he held her wrist in his hand. It was only a matter of time before she was completely his.

Thor hadn't known exactly what she looked like when he'd started this crusade. He had only been given a general description so he would know who to look for on board the ship.

She was stunning. He wanted undo her braid and run his fingers through her pale blonde hair. He needed to spread it out across his bunk. Then he wanted to strip her luscious body of her drab mourning garb and lick her all over. He would start at her ankles, and work his way up to her pretty bosom. Her breasts were plump and just large enough to fill the palms of his hands. He loved how her waist curved into a nicely rounded derriere.

Thor had a fierce need to pull her on top of him and slide inside of her tight channel. Having her wantonly ride his shaft and find pleasure remained on top of his most desired fantasies. He wanted to get her naked so he could taste every inch of her and hear her scream with satisfaction. She was everything he had ever considered to be perfect, and he could not have dreamed up a more ideal woman to find pleasure with.

He had to snap out of this line of thought. It was too early for this part of the plan, but it would happen and soon. He needed her to be a willing participant in her own downfall. He had never forced anyone in his life, and he was not about to start with his jewel. She was far beyond anything he could have expected, and he found he wanted more from her than he had originally planned. He was beginning to think he just might want to keep her forever, something he had never considered with anyone else.

He made his way topside. He needed to talk to his first mate and bosun. They needed to set a new course. They were going to make a stop in southern France instead of Calais. When he had looked through the captain's logs, he had discovered the comte had traveled to his southern estate, and that was where they would see each other again for the last time.

He needed as much time with the feisty Pia as he could manage, before they had their final meeting with her grandpere. He needed her to fall in love with him. He would use every tool in his arsenal to make that happen.

What Pia didn't know was that their lives had been forever entwined before they ever laid eyes on each other. If not for her grandpere, they would never have met. The actions of the comte ensured they would forever be linked.

Thor had to admit he was actually looking forward to getting to know her better.

He intended to have his cake, and he would savor every sweet bite.

CHAPTER FIVE

LIVING THE LIFE OF A LADY HAD MANY PERKS AND advantages. Pia had no qualms about using every one of those resources to ensure she came out on top. As an only child, Pia's father indulged all of her requests. Mr. Carlyle only had one rule he stood firm with concerning her. She could basically do anything she wanted, but if it was something he deemed dangerous, it was forbidden. Fortunately for Pia, his list of perilous things was not very long, so she pretty much ran wild on the plantation. As long as Pia was safe, her father did not object to any activity she wanted to experience.

Pia did have the benefit of a more formal education. The instructors her father hired taught her Latin, history, and math. When she wanted to learn about mythology, science, and, Greek, her father hired the best tutors he could find. She probably, in some ways, had a better education than some of the gentlemen in Charleston.

No one had a thirst for knowledge quite like Pia did. Getting lost inside the pages of a book was her favorite past time. The stories weaved lead her on adventures she couldn't have imagined herself. There were adventures to be found all from the safety of her library. As she studied with her tutors, she encountered Norse mythology and learned of the various gods. Thor had been her favorite, so it shouldn't surprise her that she was attracted to a man with the same moniker.

Her father even hired a fencing instructor when she expressed a desire to learn. He made sure the foils were dull and harmless before the lessons could commence. Pia was an apt student and excelled at everything she attempted. There was no one else more aware what her many flaws were than Pia, but she equally knew every one of her assets.

She had been locked inside his cabin for twelve days. Twelve days of doing nothing. She wanted to make sure the pirate felt at least a small amount of her frustration. Thor needed to feel it, but she had no way of accomplishing this daunting task. Pia had plenty of time and not a thing to do, except get lost inside her own mind. She could be patient, but after so long with only the pirate's occasional company, she started to slowly lose her mind. The ennui of her existence was torture only a strong person could survive. Pia questioned if she was capable of the kind of strength required to endure beyond this moment in her life.

It was beyond her comprehension why she couldn't bend Thor to her will. The pirate delivered innuendos and implied a lot, but he never acted on any of it. The more she knew about him, the less she understood what his intentions could possibly be. He made no secret that he hated her grandpere, but he failed to express how that information actually applied to her. The banter between her and Pirate Thor continued every time they were in each other's presence.

Thor remained stubborn in his desire to make her sleep next to him each night, and he absolutely refused to let her out of his cabin for any reason. Each night when he deemed it was time to rest, he made her lay down on the bunk. Once she was settled in, he would lay next to her so she could sleep inside the warmth of his embrace. It was beginning to feel safe locked in his arms as he hugged her close, her head resting above his heart. The one thing Pia knew for sure was she should not relax in his company, because it was the most dangerous place she could be.

Each night Pia experienced the same thing, and she grew more and more confused. What exactly does he have in store for me? She needed to find a way to make him talk. Well, she needed answers. He had no problem talking, but it was usually filled with innuendo. With each word he uttered, she became more confused. She wanted to hold on to her anger, but she also craved the companionship of another human being. All Thor offered her were baseless conversations leading nowhere. Pia was tired of only having him for company.

Pia was no stranger to the insinuations he alluded to every time he deigned to speak to her. She may be a woman, but she went unnoticed much growing up and had overheard men discussing their sexual exploits. Most of her knowledge was gained from books, and very few offered good illustrations of what they were talking about.

Pia had only been kissed once, when she was sixteen years old. There was a man on a neighboring plantation who thought she would be a suitable wife and had begun to court her. During a picnic at his home, he had lead her behind a tree and kissed her. It wasn't very notable, and Pia felt next to nothing, except wet and messy. What was enjoyable about a man leaving saliva all over your face? The sensation was disgusting, and his groping at her hadn't helped much. The man may have enjoyed it, but she never let him touch her again. She had doubts she would ever want to be kissed again, because the experience had been so distasteful.

She knew what desire was as she had inadvertently witnessed some clandestine meetings. Pia had just never really felt it before, and that was one of the reasons she didn't think she would ever get married. She just wasn't interested in what a man had to offer her.

That was until she came across a certain pirate. *Why do I have to feel something for a dangerous pirate?*

Losing herself in her own thought, she imagined the many things she would do to him if given the chance. They alternated between kissing him and strangling him, depending on the direction her thoughts wandered. The more she was reduced to keeping her own company, all Pia wanted to do was scream at or kill a certain pirate.

It was while she was doing her daily pacing the

pirate did the unexpected and returned to the cabin in the middle of the day. He generally left her alone until it was time to settle in for the night. Apparently being the captain of a ship kept him busy, leaving little time to entertain her.

Pia hated to admit it, but she was excited. As her only source of company, she anticipated his arrival every night. At least with him around she had someone else's voice to listen to. His presence helped keep her sanity in place. If she were left alone any more than she was, she'd have gone stark raving mad by now. Pia had reached a pinnacle in her situation, suddenly willing to give anything a try in order to have a variation in their daily routine. He wouldn't tell her how he knew her grandpere, and she was hoping to goad him into doing so.

"Ah. I see you are as busy as usual, Pia."

She glared at him, but said nothing. Pia traipsed over to the bunk and sat on the edge.

"Are you attempting to give me the silent treatment? How novel of you."

Thor sauntered over to his desk and pulled out the chair. The stool was the only piece of furniture not bolted down in the cabin. Pia watched as he sat on it and pulled himself closer to the desk. Once seated, he pulled out a key and unlocked the cabinet attached to the side of the writing table. Thor slid open the cabinet and pulled out a piece of paper, followed by a quill, and then ink. It was sad that watching him sit at his desk was entertainment to her. He made a production of setting everything on the table in preparation to write.

Pia studied the back of his head. His sun-kissed black hair was pulled back in a leather tie. It was the only way she had ever seen him wear it. Her view was blocked from seeing what he was actually doing, but she was happy just watching his shoulders move as he scribbled something across the blank pages.

When he had entered the cabin, she had been determined to ignore him, but her eyes kept being drawn back. It was too easy to watch him with an unguarded gaze. Pia felt herself wishing they could have met differently. She wanted to give in to the urge to stroke her hands over his shoulders, and it wasn't long before she started to wonder what he would do if she licked his neck.

Pia let out a whoosh of air from her lungs, and a loud sigh emerged from between her lips. She couldn't help it. The cabin was beyond tedious. If she didn't stop these fantasies about the pirate, she was going to inadvertently act out one of them. By the time the actions took place, it would be too late to change her course.

Thor was too busy to pay her any attention. Pia wanted to know more about the pirate but was unsure how to go about getting her questions answered. I simply have to find a way to get him to open up to me. No matter how many questions she asked, he never gave her any personal information about himself. Any efforts on her part to gain insight into his persona were met with little success.

Pia had little recourse but to spend time with Thor. He became the only thing occupying her thoughts. Her days started with him next to her and ended the same way. The in-between hours were spent thinking of ways to extricate herself from the situation she was in. She saw no clear way out.

Pia lay down on the bunk and tapped her fingers together while daydreams of a dashing pirate floated through her imagination. In her mind, he was really a gentleman caller approved of by her father. The dashing man courted her and asked her to be his wife. Of course she said no. Couldn't they just have an affair instead? He was shocked, but agreed to her suggestion, leading him down a pathway to sin. He was willing to do anything for her as long as she was his. Pia was such an impious girl, if only she knew what to picture that wickedness to actually be. She could guess, but she was sheltered so she didn't know.

Pia had a one track mind and these days it involved her and the pirate in various compromising situations. She stopped being terrified of him. Pia was so used to his company even the fact he towered over her became completely natural to her. She didn't understand how she could have come to be so accepting of him in such a short time.

Lost in the world of her imagination, Pia didn't realize Thor had stopped writing and was watching her. He had placed his stuff back in the cabinet, and she hadn't heard a thing. Pia often got lost in her mind and drowned out the rest of the world. The only noise that existed was the music of her own daydreams.

"Is this what you do all day?"

The pictures running through her mind made it almost impossible to hear what he had said. Unfortunately for Pia, his voice was a huge part of her daydreams so it bled through, bringing her back to reality. Choosing to ignore his question, she kept the images dancing in her mind. He was ruining my fantasy.

Irritation corded into each word as Thor spoke. "I asked you a question."

She hummed her favorite song as she imagined dancing at a ball in his arms. *Why can't he say things I want to hear?* Things like: of course I will let you go, no I didn't kill everyone on board your grandpere's ship, or how about a kiss, Pia.

Wait, she didn't want him to really do that last part, did she?

"I think that this is quite enough, Pia. I am not going to tolerate your silent treatment for much longer."

What did he expect me to say?

Pia stuck her tongue out at him in defiance.

He laughed at her as he pulled her up and off the bunk. The sound echoed across the cabin walls, amusement filling the room with each chuckle that escaped his lips.

"I think you need a lesson on some things you can do with that tongue. If you stick it out at me again, you can expect this..."

The only thought Pia had as he pulled her toward him was: be careful what you wish for.

He plundered her mouth in ways she could never have imagined. Fantasy? What fantasy? Reality was much more exciting and fulfilling. If she was capable of thought, she would have started planning on ways they could do this again.

When his tongue intertwined with hers, they danced to a tune only they could create. Any thoughts of remembering how to breathe failed to find their way into her befuddled brain. Her hands wrapped around him, and she pulled him closer. Pia felt a strong need growing inside of her. She felt Thor's hands as they roamed across the back of her head, locating the braid secured at the nape of her neck. Once he had it securely in his palms, he pulled her tresses, tipping her chin up. With her head tilted back, he placed soft kisses along her décolletage. He kissed her neckline and stopped at the base of her ears. He trailed his lips across her cheek, placing little kisses along the way, and then plundered her mouth all over again. Their tongues entwined for what seemed like hours but were no more than mere minutes. Surely there wasn't anything better than this?

He whispered in her ear. "You taste so much better than I could have imagined."

Oh he did too—so so delectable.

She enjoyed kissing him just as much, but it had to stop before she did something irreversible. She began to pull her face away from his, but he still had his arms wrapped securely around her. Pia wasn't going anywhere just yet. Thor settled her firmly against the wall of the cabin and lifted her up so her bosom was level with his mouth. His tongue found the crevice between her breasts and licked upward. He brought his mouth to hers for one last mind blowing kiss as he eased her down the wall and swung her toward the bunk.

He stepped away from Pia, putting some much needed distance between them. Pia lost her balance and fell backward onto the bed. She sat there in silence and stared at him. Words escaped her, as she had no way of describing all of the emotions flowing through her body and soul. Her mouth was swollen from his attentions, and she felt a tingling in her lower regions. Her breasts were tight and heavy, and she knew what true desire was for the first time in her life. None of the books she had read had described it with any kind of accuracy. So this is why it was forbidden.

A wide grin spread across Thor's face as he gazed at her. She felt heat stinging her cheeks, and her heart raced wildly beneath her breasts. The mirth shining in his eyes told her all she needed to know about how she appeared to him. She had been well and truly pleasured by everything he had done with his mouth and hands. What that man did with his tongue should not be permissible.

"Do you still insist on giving me the silent treatment?"

Oh yes, absolutely if you kiss me as punishment. More please, oh I am quite certain, I want you to punish me more.

Pia was equally certain she had a lot of horrible ideas lately. She was a bad girl. She needed to talk to him before he did more than kiss her breath away. He finally was doing instead of implying. Maybe, just maybe, she could get some actual information out of him. So she decided to take a nonchalant approach to the whole situation.

She shrugged. "What is there possibly to talk about?"

"Perhaps you would like to know what I have planned for you."

"Oh, you think I have finally earned the right to know that?"

He shook his head. "No Pia, dear, you won't know exactly what my plans are for you until the very last second."

There was no other person alive who could frustrate her more than her pirate. Yes, he really was her pirate in her mind. He still needed to talk about

DAWN BROWER

things that mattered to her, or she wouldn't be held accountable for her actions. With as much indignation as she could muster, Pia looked up at him. "Then why are we discussing this?"

"Because your life is going to change forever in a short time."

What an asinine statement. Pia let out an unladylike snort. Hadn't it already changed forever?

"And that is different than the past week how? Why don't we talk about you instead? Like what a murdering fiend you are for what you did too everyone on that ship."

Thor folded his arms across his chest and leaned back against his writing table. "Because my plans for you will be irreversible once everything is in place."

Damn, that didn't sound good. Pia frowned. She had to try to get him to talk more. Her life depended on what he was going to do. So she needed to do something to get him to tell her what his plans actually were.

"Seems like that is also already true, what could be so different today? One thing is certain, you are very good at evading questions. Why don't you tell me why you needed to kill everyone aboard my grandpere's ship?"

"I never told you I killed everyone on that ship. You just assumed I did."

"An assumption that you never corrected. You wanted me to believe the worst in you."

Thor shrugged. "It suited my purposes at the time."

"So are you going to tell me anything else, since you are in such a sharing mood today?" Pia inquired.

"I grow weary of your persistent questioning. I have answered all you need to know for now."

"You answered nothing, you only implied you didn't kill anyone, much the same way that you insinuated you murdered a whole ship of people."

"Believe what you want Pia. The truth will be evident when it matters. I don't need to confirm or deny anything."

"Okay, I'm tired of your non-answers. Why did you come in here to bother me?"

"We will be making port in a couple of days. You will be able to come on deck. Once you are topside you will agree to everything I ask you to do. No matter what it is you will do it. If you don't, I will personally make sure that your only living family member dies."

"Are you saying you would murder my grandpere?"

Thor leaned down and looked her directly in her eyes his intentions crystal clear as he enunciated each syllable. "In a heartbeat."

Pia didn't want to think he would kill her grand-pere. It just didn't make sense to her why he would do something so evil to someone she loved. "I don't believe you. Why not threaten my life?"

"Because it's clear you have no regard for your own life. I figured, if I threatened someone you love, then you would be more willing to follow my lead and do as I say. It also helps that I have a deep hatred for your grandpere. His death is nothing at all to me."

He had her there. She would die before she let him control her. Her grandpere though? Pia had to protect him.

"You are despicable."

"You enjoy it though, love. I could have done whatever I wanted to you earlier, and you would have followed me to hell and back. You were so hot, you seared my skin. Maybe talking with you isn't the best use of my time? In the future, I'll just show you what I want instead."

Without thinking, Pia slapped Thor across his left cheek.

Thor's amusement still hung in the air. His

laugher echoed through the cabin as he sauntered out of the room.

Pia had a lot to think about. Would the pirate actually kill her grandpere? She believed he would. He made sure she knew he harbored no tender feelings for her grandpere. Oh yes, Pirate Thor would follow through with his threat to kill the comte. He left her little choice. If she wanted to ensure her only living family member remained alive, she would have to do everything he asked of her, even if she hated every minute of it. The only option Pia had was to pray she could actually follow through with whatever plans he had in store.

HE HAD ALMOST GONE TOO FAR with Pia. If he had stayed there even a moment longer, he would have ravished her completely. He needed her, and as he got to know her, his plans changed course, moving in a completely different direction.

She was supposed to fall in love with him. He had blundered a bit there. He would have to make her forget he had threatened her grandpere's life somehow. Not that Comte Dubois didn't deserve to die. He was an evil man. If not for him, Thor would never have become a pirate. But that also meant he would never have met Pia. Thor's conundrum was his constant craving for Pia. It hadn't been in his plans to want her as much as he did.

He had intended to offer her some of the things from her trunks. It was clear to him she was restless. Thor would offer her a boon the next time he talked to her. Peace was important to have between them. It did not bode well with his plans to always be so overbearing and obnoxious with her. Although, she did appear to enjoy being kissed.

He walked up to the deck to check their progress. They should be in Bordeaux in less than two days. His plans would be in full motion once they were in port with the anchor dropped. When it was all done, he would be able to have what he wanted most. Revenge. Thor would also have something he was starting to desire almost more than that. Almost.

When he got topside, he located his first mate to make sure they were on schedule. Jamieson was at the bow of the ship with his sextant measuring the angles on the horizon.

"Are we on our scheduled course, Jamieson?"

"We are, Captain."

"Excellent work. Let me know if we run into any

problems. I don't want to have anything spoil the plans I've made."

"Aye aye, Captain."

Thor walked away making his way to the galley. With his cabin occupied by a tempting beauty, he couldn't spend his leisure time there. He would make the cook get out his bottle of scotch and pour him a glass.

He was desperately in need of something to assist him while slumbering alongside Pia in their shared bunk. It would prove difficult to find any rest lying next to her later that night in his current state. Thor hoped the alcohol would help him pass out and prevent him from groping her...much.

CHAPTER SIX

THOR STARTED TO SPECULATE ABOUT LIFE AND THE choices he made. A person's existence could become their own version of hell on Earth. Sadly he knew more about that than anyone else did. The choices he made often demanded every ounce of his blood, sweat, and tears. The very essence of his soul had been devoured whole, chewed, and spit out with nothing good remaining to maintain its life force. His soul remained on the brink of being lost, never to be retrieved again. At the same time life is inherently full of surprises at every turn, both good and bad depending on which path is chosen. The course he selected determined how much of his soul was beyond redemption or if it had one last chance to achieve salvation.

Watching the sun rise above the ocean announcing a new day, Thor thought of all of the reasons he set himself on this particular path. Revenge was the course of action he had taken, and he couldn't extricate himself from it even if he wanted to.

Pia was a revelation he had not anticipated. When he had heard she was traveling to live with Comte Dubois, all he could see was a way to enact his vengeance. The reality of it all was more of a shock than having his partner put a bullet through his shoulder. He was beginning to need her. He knew he had to alter his course before he crossed a line.

The port of Bordeaux beckoned him. Some plans already set in motion were irrevocable. Once the anchor dropped, he would need to make some quick alterations to his plans. In the missive he had written in front of Pia, those changes would be hastened. He just needed to send one of his crew to deliver the message of their arrival, and once it was done, everything should go smoothly.

His heart would never recover if he lost it all because he couldn't correct some of the mistakes he had already made. As it was, there was still a lot that was unforgivable. Sadly events to come might hamper any effort he made. Pia was still an essential part of his plan, but the difference was how she would be used in his revenge.

He still needed to make sure the comte paid for his treachery. The modification was in how much of it would destroy the humanity that remained of his soul. What he was doing to gain retribution wouldn't blacken him to the core. It was something he could, and would, happily live with. Some things were worth whatever price needed to be paid. This was one time there would be no regrets. There were times when he thought he would never be able to make Renny Dubois pay for his betrayal, and it was finally within his grasp. He just had to reach out and take it. He was so lost in thought he hadn't heard his bosun approach until he started to speak.

"Captain we are almost to the harbor of Bordeaux. I have Timmy getting ready to take a dinghy to shore. Is your message ready?"

Thor pulled out the missive. He had carefully written all of his instructions on the day he'd gotten his first taste of Pia. She had been so occupied with her own thoughts she hadn't even been curious about what he had been writing. At first that had disappointed him until he turned around and saw the expression on her face.

There had been such a look of longing in her eyes as she chewed her bottom lip. He lost control when her tongue slowly rolled over her lips leaving them a shiny invitation to be kissed. He couldn't restrain himself after that. He had to taste her. It was nice to see a lighter side of her personality emerge. If she had never stuck her tongue out at him, he may never have given in to his desire to kiss her.

He rolled the missive between his fingers remembering how much that day had transformed his outlook. His needs had altered so much because of that one moment of weakness. He wouldn't go back and change any part of that day, even knowing how much it would change him or what it forced him to admit about himself. After spending the past two weeks with Pia, he knew she was meant to be his. That day had sealed it for him. Thor turned to his bosun and handed him the message.

"Tell Timmy to wait for the reverend and bring all our guests back with him. The crew and I will await their arrival. Also, make sure he is aware I would like them here as quickly as possible. I want to have enough time to make sure Pia is back below deck before the sun sets tonight. It will be too dangerous to allow her to remain on deck after the ceremony."

"I will make sure that Timmy follows your directions, sir. After all it is a good night for a celebration."

Thor laughed. "It is indeed, Corny. It is indeed."

"The cook also wanted me to let you know that tonight's meal would be remembered for a long time to come. We got quite a haul from the galley of the ship we plundered, including a nice case of brandy and scotch. He wants to know if you'd like us to break it open for the celebration tonight."

"I think that's a fine plan, Corny. Also, any unnecessary crew can have shore leave for the night. Tell them they can go after tonight's celebration and remind them they need to be back on the ship before sunset tomorrow night. We will set sail after everyone's returned."

"Aye aye, Captain. I will take care of everything."

Thor found himself smiling in anticipation. Soon he would have everything he desired, including the alluring Pia. Her charms were something he ached to sample. After the blazing kisses they had shared, he knew her desire was equal to his. Pia was full of a fire that would consume with the right amount of fuel feeding her flames. It would be his honor and pleasure to share that bliss with her. After the ceremony just before dusk, she would be his in every way. Once the formalities were out of the way, they could explore what made each other burn.

IF PIA DIDN'T STOP WALKING BACK and forth, she was bound to wear a hole in the cabin floor, clear through to the cargo hold. If that damn pirate showed his face today, she was going to pummel it with her fists. He needed to let her out of this cabin. He could at least have given her something to read. Then again, he did have that locked cabinet.

Staring at the cabinet as if seeing it for the first time, she analyzed it for weaknesses. Maybe it is possible to unlock it. With little to amuse herself, she was desperate enough to try anything. She scoured the room, looking for a tool that could help her pry it open. She turned the bunk inside out, throwing things on the floor. The blankets and pillows hit the ground with a soft thud. There was nothing there. She pulled the mattress up and pushed it against the wall. She looked beneath it. When she did not find anything of use, she let it flop back down haphazardly on top of its wooden frame. She turned and spotted the pirate's trunk. Rushing over to it, she tried to lift the top with her bare hands. The bloody thing was locked too, and she kicked it in frustration.

Nothing. There was nothing in the room. This was the worst torture ever imagined. She moved over to the cabinet to see if she could pry it open with her hands.

Pia kept trying to tear it open unaware that Thor had entered. He watched her for several seconds before he spoke. "Perhaps I could help you with that?"

Pia jumped back, startled by his voice next to her. "Must you be so damned quiet?"

A chuckle rumbled out of his chest, developing into a full blown laugh. It was like a bolt of lightning striking the ground and spreading a light through a dark room.

"It was not my intention. I can see you have idle hands. Perhaps, I can give you something to keep them busy."

"Really? What? Do you have any books? I would love to have something to read. It would go a long way in curing the chronic boredom I've developed while being held captive."

"Sadly, pirates have little use for books. We don't have time for any leisurely pursuits. I might have a map or two you could entertain yourself with, but that wasn't exactly what I had in mind."

"I am almost afraid to ask. What exactly do you have in mind?"

"Well we could always continue where we left off the other day. That wall there was quiet handy in keeping you in place and what you were doing with your hands—purely inspirational."

Pia glared at him. Is he serious? Please let him be serious. She wanted to kiss him again and feel his hands roaming over her body. She wanted him to suck her nipples and squeeze her breasts. Wait, where did that idea come from? It was a fine idea indeed, and it needed to happen. I really, really need it to happen. She was about to make her demands when she remembered she was supposed to discourage such actions. She had to be sensible, and the pirate had already proven his kisses made her brainless.

"That is not what I had in mind and you know it."

"Pia, love, you are the most amusing woman I have ever encountered. I can see the conflicting emotions all over your face. No worries, my dear, I do have something else in mind. I thought perhaps you would enjoy a bath and a change of clothes."

She raised an eyebrow. "Is this some kind of trick? What's the catch?"

"No trick or catch. I want you to be comfortable and feel your best today. We are having a celebration tonight, and you will be able to come on deck."

"Really? I can leave the cabin now? I'd been starting to think you were lying about allowing me out of this blasted room."

"Yes, for an hour or so. Your attendance at the celebration is much desired."

"Then yes, absolutely, I would love a bath. But, I don't have any underclothes or another dress that I can put on when I'm done."

"Don't worry. I'll make sure you have something besides that drab dress you choose to wear."

"Are you serious? It isn't like you have given me a change of attire since I have been on your ship."

"I didn't have a reason to before. I was commenting more on your choice of attire, period. It's dreadful, and you need to wear something with more color. Black, my dear, does nothing for you."

"I'm in mourning, my father died. That's what you wear to honor the dead."

"I know. All the same, you will no longer wear black. I don't like it."

Pia pursed her lips together, letting her displeasure be known. She looked at Thor. "All right, Captain. As I have no choice but to follow your dictates, I guess I will have to agree if I want a bath and a change of clothes."

He smiled at her, and she felt her heart flutter faster. Damn him and his alluring smile. It should be illegal, not that it would stop him. He was a pirate after all. They never followed any laws, unless they were of their own making. If there was one thing Pia was more than aware of, it was that this particular pirate made his own rules. This ship was a nation of its own making. Any regulations were enforced by the one and only sovereign pirate, Thor.

"As always, Pia, you make things more interesting. I will send my cabin boy up with your hot water. Do not give him any trouble. If you try to leave the cabin before you are supposed to, you will regret it. Take this small peace offering and enjoy your bath."

Pia sighed. "I can't very well argue with your logic."

"Of course you can't, it won't take you long to realize that I am generally right in most situations. One more thing before I go, please clean up the mess you made before Gus comes with your bath. I know that you didn't have anything to do, but tearing the cabin apart isn't an acceptable form of entertainment. It wouldn't do very well for us to sleep on wet things tonight."

He turned and walked out the door, making sure it was secured behind him. Once it was closed, Pia stuck her tongue out at him. She didn't dare do it to his face any more. Even if she wanted him to kiss her again, she couldn't allow it to happen. They almost went too far the last time.

After reflecting on her situation, she didn't think it was wise to get too attached to the pirate. He was undoubtedly handsome and his kiss was an experience she would always treasure, but her heart would break if she allowed him to have it. She did not believe it was possible for her to have an affair without letting herself feel something for the other person. She had already begun to care about the pirate, and all they had done was kiss.

Pia sighed and looked at the room. She had made quite a mess of the small cabin. On this one occasion she conceded that Thor had a point. The room's current chaotic state needed to be set to rights. She had no idea how long it would be before her bath was brought to the cabin so she immediately began to clean up the room. It didn't take her long to put everything back where it belonged and decided she needed a break from the exertion.

Pia was lying on the bunk when the door opened. She turned to see a boy of no more than twelve come in carrying a wooden tub. He placed it near the bunk and walked out of the room. He wasn't much of a conversationalist.

Pia got up to inspect the tub. It wasn't very large. Looking at it, she wondered how anyone larger than her could possibly fit inside of it. She wondered where the captain got the tub, and if he had intended for her to bathe all along. Where did the rest of them bathe? Did they even bother?

It wasn't long before the boy returned. This time he was carrying two large buckets of steaming water. He quickly poured them into the tub. When he was done, he looked over at her and set the buckets down.

"Miss, I will be back with more hot water. Once the tub is half full, then a couple of pails with cooler water will be available so you can make it to your liking. I'm to bring you some soap and drying cloths as well. After I bring you everything, you are free to take your bath. I just wanted to let you know so that you can bathe in peace."

"Thank you, what's your name?"

"Gus, ma'am."

"Thank you, Gus. Are you bringing me a change of clothes too?"

"I don't rightly know, ma'am. I suspect the captain has everything you need ready, and you will get it when he decides you need it."

"Hmm. Of course he does. Thank you again, Gus."

Odious man.

When Gus left, Pia silently fumed. Give it to her when he wants her to have it, will he. It was time to share her frustrations with him. Thor had no idea how much he drove her insane. The pirate would soon learn exactly what Pia's capabilities were. This was definitely going to be an amusing day.

Gus continued to fill her bath. He completed his task efficiently, working as fast as his small frame could manage. Once he was gone, she didn't waste any time because the water would cool and make her bath a miserable experience. She adjusted the water to her desired temperature. While she was finishing that task, Gus came in one last time with a couple stacks of dry cloths and a bar of soap.

"Here be your soap, ma'am. I will be by later to

collect the water and tub. I will knock first so as to make sure you're decent."

Pia looked over as Gus left the room. The door shut with a quiet click. She heard the key turn, locking her inside once again. She began to undress, and it wasn't until he left that she realized she had a dilemma. *How the heck am I going to get my corset off?*

CHAPTER SEVEN

THOR HAD DECIDED HE NEEDED TO GIVE PIA something to occupy her time with. When he had walked in earlier and found the cabin a mess with her attempting to yank open his cabinet, he knew she was at her wit's end. So he dug through one of her trunks, locating some books for her. He had heard her expound at length about how much she loved every one of her damned books. Apparently, she really loved mythology. So it was with some amusement he picked up a book titled: Thor, God of Thunder. He couldn't wait to see the look on her face when he handed it to her. Yes, he was attempting to do her a favor, but that didn't mean he couldn't find humor in giving her that book just to get a reaction out of her.

When Thor walked into the cabin, he found Pia struggling to untie her corset. Thor leaned on the frame of the doorway and watched her with amusement. He let out a laugh that echoed throughout the cabin like a roll of thunder, much like the god he was named after. The boisterous sound succeeded in gaining her attention.

Pia glanced back at him briefly only to turn back around, still struggling to loosen her stays. "I'm glad I can amuse you. What are you doing here anyway? I thought I had privacy to bathe?" She waved her hands motioning him to come to her. "Never mind, make yourself useful and untie this blasted thing. I don't have a maid, as you left her on the other ship, so you can act in her place."

Her face was turned away as she stood quietly with her back to him. Thor took his packages and set them on the table. He walked over and pulled at the laces of her corset, loosening them. He leaned over her shoulder, his breath hot on her neck and whispered in her ear. "Oh, I assure you I have no problem acting as your maid. I have wanted to undress you for days."

"How crude, just unlace this thing. Then you can leave. Did you bring me a change of clothes? Forget the corset. I am not wearing it again. I don't have a maid to help with the blasted thing. It's far too much to deal with on my own."

Thor laughed as he listened to her ramble on without giving him a chance to respond. Pia talked so fast it was impossible to get a word in. Once she stopped to take a breath, Thor took the opportunity to speak.

"It was good of you to remember to straighten up the mess you made earlier. I did remember how agitated you were and thought perhaps you would like one of the books from your trunks. Yes, I did remember your clothes. They were especially made for you. I hope the dress pleases you."

"Wait, you have my trunks? Why didn't you tell me this sooner? There are things in there I could use. Why wouldn't you let me have my things?" she demanded. Her agitation showed as Pia swung her hands around in circular motion, emphasizing her disapproval through the movement.

"I didn't see any reason before now."

"I don't know why I'm surprised. Nothing you do shocks me anymore, just leave the stuff on the table and leave so I can bathe in peace."

"I have no intention of leaving."

"I beg your pardon?"

Thor raised an eyebrow, mocking her. It was clear he had her backed into a corner. She could not find a way to extricate herself from. He didn't budge on anything once he set his mind to it. Thor knew Pia would acquiesce to his demands.

"Well, love, it is as simple as this. I am going to go take a little nap over there on the bunk. I'm weary and want to rest before tonight's celebration. I won't bother you while you bathe. Go ahead and do as you planned."

Pia stared at him with her mouth gaping. Shock riddled her face, turning it a bright shade of red. It would be interesting to see what she would do. He was actually looking forward to it. He loved teasing her.

Thor watched as she reached down to check the temperature of the bath water. The water had a little steam billowing over the tub as she ran her fingers over it. Seeming to be satisfied with the temperature, she grabbed the soap and a dry cloth and set them near the tub. Her pantaloons and chemise hit the floor, leaving her completely naked before him. Her pert backside was in full view as she climbed into the tub keeping her back to him the entire time. It took everything he had not to walk over, pull her back out of the tub, and explore every inch of her body. Instead, he laid there in silence and watched as she scrubbed her body clean. Pia poured a bucket of water over her head to rinse herself off. When the water flowed over her head dousing every inch of her, Thor's eyes remained on her back as tiny droplets of water slowly trailed down the curve of her spine.

She was completely thorough in her bathing, washing every inch of herself. Thor was entranced as she slowly brought a washcloth across her neck and it disappeared from his view, down toward her bosom. He had never been so jealous of a piece of cloth in his life. He wanted to touch everything it brushed against. The longer he lay there watching her, the harder he got beneath his trousers. Siren's were fabled to tempt sailors to their doom. Pia could very well be one put on Earth to bring about his demise. The beautiful temptress scrubbing her skin pink in front of him was surely created to torture him with pleasure.

It took every ounce of his will not to strip his clothes off and pull her out of that blasted tub. His need for her grew with every breath he took. Thor assured himself he would have her soon. He could be patient and wait for the appropriate time. Thor gritted his teeth in frustration as he rubbed a hand over his aching member.

Yes, he was going to be inside her and soon. The little minx was begging him by bathing before him. No lady would have done so unless she secretly desired a man's attentions. In the evening, if all went as planned, Pia would have his complete attention. He just had to bide his time and survive this torturous experience. In the meantime, he intended to enjoy the show she provided for him.

"Pia, love, must you make so much noise splashing the water? I am trying to relax over here."

"Yes. If you have a problem with it, you can leave."

"I don't know. If you are going to be so loud, maybe I should just enjoy the scenery."

He was trying to goad her. It wasn't working. Pia just kept scrubbing her skin and removing the dirt. She was in the bath for thirty minutes before it became clear she was done. There was nothing left on her alabaster skin to scrub clean. She had cleansed her body so much that every inch had turned a delightful pink. Her skin glowed from all of her ministrations. If Thor were to hazard a guess, everything Pia did was for his benefit. He was certain she was trying her best to torture him, and he couldn't let her know it was working.

Pia slowly turned her head, impishness shining in her eyes as she looked over at Thor. "Was the scenery to your liking?"

"Immensely."

Her head turned slightly so he could see the outline of her profile. Pia's voice was husky as she replied. "Hmm. Well, I wonder if there is a way to improve on that."

"I'm sure you can think of something."

"Oh, I am intelligent enough. I'm sure I could be creative as well."

It was Thor's turn to smile. He had no doubt she could be creative. He couldn't wait to find out how resourceful she could be. "I have no doubt that you could do anything."

She gave him something to look at—and he lost his cocksure smile too.

WITH THAT, Pia stood and turned to face him. The droplets of water trailed between the valley of her breasts, creating a path toward her belly button. The small rivulet flowed even farther south. Thor's eyes tracked every inch of the course it made.

Thor got up and walked over to the table where the dry cloths were placed. He grabbed one and tossed it at her. If he didn't get away from her, he was going to lick every particle of water off of her body like a man desperate for a drink. Just looking at her made him salivate.

"Please be a dear, dry yourself off, and get dressed. The celebration is scheduled to start in an hour. I'll be back then to collect you."

He managed to remain cool and aloof as he walked toward the cabin door. Once outside, he quickly secured the lock. Thor rested his head on the door and took a deep breath. That was too close. He had almost given in and ruined all of his plans.

While she stood there dripping water all over the cabin floor, Thor had been struck dumb. The sneaky, sensual wench had effectively turned the tables on him. Thor had never been a betting man and wouldn't gamble his plans away at this juncture of the operation, at least at this stage when their relationship hadn't gone beyond a few kisses. He couldn't take any chances that his carefully laid plans might fall to pieces if he gave in to Pia's charms too early.

She was every fantasy brought to life. The beautiful, wet witch had done something he'd never expected. If he wasn't already in deep, that little scene would've told him one thing. He'd willingly jump into shark infested waters to claim her as his own. He'd finally found a woman who was his equal in every way.

CHAPTER EIGHT

PIA STILL HELD THE DRYING CLOTH THOR HAD TOSSED at her. Her hand rose to grab it out of the air as he exited the room. Pia automatically began to dry herself with the towel. Could that have been any more embarrassing? He appeared to be upset with her. Why? She thought she had read the signs correctly. Thor wanted her. His body gave that away whenever he pressed himself against her.

She felt his hard shaft pressing against her derriere as they slept each night. Its length growing as he spooned against her, holding her in his tight embrace. While in her presence, it appeared as if the pirate was hard all the time. Why did he act like I just insulted him? She may be naïve, but she knew what a man's body did when he desired a woman. Pia didn't understand why Thor had damn near run out of the room. His desire was evident by the look in his eyes. So why did he feel the need to put distance between them?

She looked through the items he had brought for her. There was a clean chemise, pantaloons, a brush, and some blue hair ribbons. But the jewel in the treasure trove was the royal blue dress that matched her eyes. The bodice was lower than she would have liked, but it looked like it would hug her every curve. It was made of the softest silk and trimmed with the finest lace. He didn't bring her any matching slippers, so she would have to make do with her sensible travel shoes. Why did he bring me something so fine and beautiful to wear?

She quickly put on her new chemise and pantaloons. Once she was partially dressed, she traipsed over and sat on the chair by the table. She grabbed the brush and untangled the knots already forming in her long blonde mane. Pia hummed a happy tune as her nimble fingers created a simple braid and laced one of the blue ribbons through it. After the braid was completed, she took another ribbon and tied it off at the end to make sure it stayed in place. After her hair was arranged to her liking, she pulled on her stockings.

Pia picked up her dress and stepped into it, pulling it up. Luckily the gown laced in the front, making it easier for her to put on without the assistance of a maid. All of her other ensembles hooked in the back. With her gown securely fastened, Pia walked over and grabbed her shoes off the floor. She sat on the edge of the bed so it would be easier to slip them onto her feet. Once she had them in place, Pia laced them firmly. She stood and smoothed the dress with her hands so it fell in even waves down to the floor.

The door opened, and Pia looked up as Thor entered the room. He had always been attractive, but in that instant, she was amazed at how good he really looked. To say he was handsome did not do him justice. He was breathtaking.

He had clearly taken the time to bathe. As usual, his beautiful onyx hair was pulled back in a leather tie. He was dressed in his finest pirate attire. He wore black leather pants that hugged his thighs, making it possible to see every inch of his body. His pearly white shirt billowed over his shoulders and was tucked into his trousers. His tan skin gleamed against the stark white of his tunic. Thor's eyes held a mischievous twinkle that made Pia a little nervous about this supposed celebration.

Thor took his time looking over Pia as he circled around her with an appreciative scrutiny. Once he had made a full circle, he stopped in front of her. "Ah good, you are ready."

"Well you did tell me I would be able to leave the cabin today. I wasn't going to delay that for any reason."

A small chuckle escaped him and reverberated through the room. A roguish smile slowly formed on his lips. "Very true, love. Come along, I have a lot of surprises for you."

"Can I have a hint?"

"Only a small one. It is something you could never guess."

Pia stuck her tongue out at him. "You call that a hint?"

"Careful, Pia, you remember what happened the last time you stuck your tongue out at me."

Pia looked at Thor with an impish grin. "Oh, I remember that quite well. I just figured you must have gotten your needs taken care of elsewhere. You didn't seem interested in touching me earlier."

Thor raised an eyebrow at her, amusement shining in his eyes as he looked down at her.

"Nothing could be further from the truth. I like to savor my treats, and make no mistake about it, you would be a treat. There wasn't enough time to enjoy you earlier."

It was Pia's turn to raise her eyebrow. As far as she was concerned, he already had his chance and blew it. She didn't believe in unwarranted second chances. So she told him the truth as she saw it. "Well, it was a onetime offer. One that has already expired, so it won't be an issue since you're not going to touch me again."

"Be careful about issuing me commands. You will soon realize that I'm the only one in charge."

"Right." Pia rolled her eyes. "Because you are the mighty Pirate Thor."

"Absolutely, it's best you don't forget that. Come. Our guests await us."

THOR ESCORTED PIA to the quarterdeck. It was kind of nice to stroll along with her. She looked ravishing in the blue dress, but he couldn't wait to get her out of it. They had been spending all of their time in his cabin. This was a different way to see her and enjoy her company. This celebration had been planned for weeks. As soon as the intel had come to him she would be crossing the ocean to live with her grand-pere in France, he knew what he had to do. Comte Dubois was the one responsible for the life he now led. He would never have been a pirate if the man hadn't tried to execute him. This was his chance to pay the comte back in kind. He would have his precious granddaughter for his own, and the comte wouldn't be able to do anything to stop him. His plan was brilliant.

"Do you remember the conversation we had a few days ago?"

"You will have to clarify which conversation. We have had many."

Thor looked at her with delight shining in his eyes. Conversing with Pia was a game he would never tire of. His voice held a tinge of devilment. "Don't play coy Pia, you know what I'm talking about. I am referring to when we discussed the day you would be allowed to come on deck. Please don't disappoint me. I'm sure you'll enjoy some company other than mine, even if it's brief."

"Ah, the one where you said I had to follow all of your orders, or you would kill my grandpere."

"Yes, that one. If you do not do everything I ask of you, I will kill your grandpere."

With a petulant smile, Pia looked up at him. "I understand. You do not have to remind me of that."

"Excellent. I'm glad you're on board with the plan, because I have an extra special surprise for you. Well a couple of surprises, I hope they please you. Don't leave my side for any reason. I promise, you will regret it if you do."

Thor wished reminding her he would kill her grandpere wasn't a necessary evil, but he needed her to comply with everything he had planned. It was unfortunate they had to meet this way. She really was perfect for him. In a very short time, she had become the most important person in his life. He sincerely wished they could have met at a different time.

Life had sent him on a path, and he hadn't been given a choice. He had learned to embrace it as the tool that would eventually give him the revenge he sought.

His Pia was beautiful, but more importantly, she was also feisty and smart. He had a feeling she would always be able to surprise him. It was his deepest wish to have her with him all the time so she could continue to astonish him for the rest of their lives. So it was with a heavy heart he continued on his chosen path, hoping that one day she would be able to forgive him for what he felt must be done.

"I already told you I would do what you ask. You don't need to remind me again," Pia said as she stopped. "Is that my grandpere?"

Thor had been walking her toward where Comte Dubois was standing, guarded by several of his crew. He had been brought to the ship by one of the pirate crew. Comte Dubois was a man of average height, an olive complexion, and dark ebony hair dusted with grey. He was stout and had a small pouch of a belly, showing how comfortable he was getting as he aged. Everything was coming together nicely. Thor couldn't wait to see the reaction on the comte's face when he married his granddaughter.

"How did my grandpere get here, Thor?" Pia demanded.

"Thor? Pieretta you are mistaken. This man's name is not Thor." Comte Dubois told his granddaughter.

Pia stood looking at Thor in shocked silence. She tilted her head at him, confusion clouding her face. Thor knew she wanted to know what was going on, and the answers she needed from him would become apparent momentarily. His gaze was firmly on Comte Dubois as he responded to his statement.

"Your grandpere would know exactly who I am, Pia. He did try to murder me after all."

"I did not try to murder you. I was trying to save you. Standing directly behind you was a pirate, and he was aiming his pistol straight at you. When I fired mine, I was aiming at him."

"Really, Renny, you expect me to believe you shot me while trying to save me? Then why did you leave me there to die?"

"I did no such thing. I went to get help. By the time I came back, you were gone."

Thor raised an eyebrow in disbelief. "So you took it as a sign I had died? You rushed to have me declared dead so you could gain control over our business. I'm actually amazed they took your word for it. There was very little evidence of my supposed demise."

Thor kept a close eye on Pia throughout his exchange with Comte Dubois. He saw the confusion spread over her features. She looked back and forth between the two of them, her face growing paler with each statement.

Looking directly into Thor's eyes, Pia asked. "Who are you really? Grandpere says your name is not Thor. I want your real name."

Thor shrugged his shoulders, dismissing what

the comte had told her. The comte didn't really know him or the name his loved ones had known him by. He looked down at her. "Thor is my name."

"That's a lie. His name is William Thorston Marsden, Fifth Viscount Torrington," Comte Dubois shouted.

"He is correct. I go by a shortened version of my second name. Thor is short for Thorston. I was named after my father, and my mother wanted me to have my own identity. To my family and close friends I was always Thor. You wouldn't have known that, Renny. You always referred to me by my title. I was always Torrington to you. Did that make it easier to murder me? Was it more impersonal that way?"

"I told you I didn't try to kill you, Torrington," Comte Dubois insisted.

Thor had listened to enough of the comte's lies. It was time to end the charade and finish everything once and for all. He wanted the comte off of his ship and out of his life for good. He looked at the man with contempt, distaste filling his mouth from spending time in his malicious company. If his presence wasn't so important to fulfilling his vengeance, the comte would not be aboard, talking to them. He waved his hand at him dismissively.

"No matter, I don't care. That is not why you're here."

"What do you want with me then?"

Thor looked at him. "I couldn't very well marry Pia without her only family being present to witness the union now could I?"

Thor heard Pia gasp. He knew it was a shock to her. He didn't think she would have agreed if he had outright asked her. They certainly didn't have a traditional relationship by any means.

When he had kidnapped her, his original plan had been to seduce her and return her to Renny as soiled goods. The more time he spent with her, the more apparent it became he couldn't do that to her. He knew he could never do that. This was the only choice he had if he was going to keep her safe with him. He needed to make her his wife. It was not in his makeup to just willingly hand her over to her grandpere and hope for the best. No, this is what must be done.

Comte Dubois started to spit and sputter at Thor's announcement. His voice filled with uncontrollable rage as he screamed. "You are not marrying my granddaughter, Torrington."

A wicked smile crossed Thor's lips. "I absolutely am. Pia consented to be with me for the rest of her life. I wanted to make sure she didn't have any regrets. It is part of the reason I made sure you were present. Ah, here is the priest now, it's time to begin."

THE CEREMONY WENT by in a blur. She didn't even remember saying I do. She couldn't believe Thor wanted to marry her. She was still confused by it all. He wouldn't let her go near her grandpere. He said her grandpere was too dangerous, and he wouldn't allow her to ever be around someone so evil. Here she was, married to a pirate viscount of all things, and she would never be allowed to see her family again.

This was why she never wanted to get married. Men had all of the control. Thor had threatened her grandpere's life. If she didn't marry him, he would have killed her grandpere. With the comte standing on the deck, the threat had seemed very real to her. He begged her to not marry Thor. Pia could tell he didn't understand why she was going through with it when he shook his head in confusion. Grandpere didn't know she was only marrying Thor to protect him. She couldn't be held responsible for his death.

Please let my grandpere be okay.

Her feelings for her pirate were complicated. They had spent only a short time together on board his ship, but Pia believed she had begun to understand him. In some ways, she felt she knew him more than she knew herself.

This whole situation felt wrong in so many ways. Marrying Thor turned her life even farther upside down. It sank deeper and deeper into a never-ending fiasco, one she could never escape. Why did he want to marry me? He attacked a ship and kidnapped me to make me his wife? Pia shook her head in confusion. Why would that matter?

Once it was all over, Thor had escorted Pia back to their cabin. Before he closed the door, he had informed her he would be back in an hour or so. He had some things to take care of on deck. Thor had looked at her directly in the eyes and said he was looking forward to spending the night with his new wife. When he left, she thought she'd be lucky if he actually gave her that much time.

She had done everything Thor had asked of her. One thing was for sure, Pia had a lot of questions, and Thor was going to answer them all. She had never wanted a husband. Thor had effectively tied her hands, making it the only decision she could make.

Pia had longed to be an independent woman. Thor took that away from her by forcing her to marry him. She wasn't exactly delighted to be his blushing bride. It didn't really matter because regardless of how she felt about the situation, Thor was her husband now. She wasn't going to back down. He would do what she wanted for once.

CHAPTER NINE

THOR KNEW HE HAD TO FACE HIS BRIDE SOONER rather than later. Unfortunately, it was several hours before he was able to get away from the crew to seek her out. After he ensured Comte Dubois and the priest were back on shore, he could deal with the ramifications of the day's events. Some of his crew had been worried the comte might try and come back on board to harm him. So he had to assure them it was okay to go ahead with the shore leave he granted them. He wanted them to have some time to themselves before they set sail again.

Thor made his way to the cabin to deal with his new wife. He was prepared for a temper tantrum. In fact, he was looking forward to it. He liked when she got mad and feisty. It made things a lot more interesting.

He wasn't prepared to explain everything to her just yet. He wanted to show her everything he wanted from her first. He yearned to express all the bottled up desire and longing he had been holding back. Thor wasn't always good with words and often found actions were a much better way of getting his point across. They would have to talk eventually, but he was hoping to put it off for as long as possible. For now, Thor wanted her to feel everything he was feeling. He needed to experience what it was like to be inside of her. He patiently waited until he could love her the only way he knew how.

Pia was his wife, and he finally had the right to explore every inch of her luscious body. She had given him a very brazen invitation after her bath earlier that evening. It hadn't been the proper time to accept it, but he was more than ready now that they were legally wed.

He walked into the cabin and was surprised to find Pia asleep on the bunk. She had taken off her dress and draped it over the chair by the table. Thor stopped to stare at Pia for a while, admiring her beauty. Her chest rose and fell with an even pace.

She was utterly and completely beautiful. To him she was perfect, but more importantly...she was his.

Thor removed his boots, and the rest of his clothes followed shortly after. He crawled onto the bunk with his wife. Her instinct made her curl next to him. She was used to sleeping with him and didn't rouse when he pulled her closer. He slowly caressed her, hoping she would awaken. He needed her conscious for every part of the loving he was going to give her.

PIA WAS HAVING the best dream. It felt so real. She was almost afraid to open her eyes and discover it wasn't. She didn't want it to stop. Phantom hands wandered down her body. She felt light kisses across her cheek and trail down her neck. The warmth spread all over her body, increasing with each new sensation. Her body had never felt so amazing from such simple contact with another person. Wait, there really is someone's lips floating over my body, drowning it with kisses.

Her eyes flew open, and she found Thor staring into them.

"Good of you to wake up, love."

"What are you doing, Thor?"

"I'm loving my wife."

If Pia had been capable of snorting at that moment, she would have. He claimed her grandpere was the master of lies, and here falsehoods spilled from his lips. Both Thor and her grandpere expected her to believe them, but she didn't really know either one of them. She wanted a real conversation with her grandpere, but Thor would never allow that to happen. It was up to her to find a way.

In the meantime, she had to deal with Thor's amorous intentions. He said he was going to love her. She didn't believe he actually loved her in any way, shape, or form. But he did desire her, and as her husband, he would want to express it. Fortunately for him, she equally desired him, and she might as well get something out of this sham of a marriage. Her gaze drifted up to meet his. "You do not love me, Thor. I am just a pawn in your revenge against my grandpere."

"Nevertheless, we are going to find pleasure in each other."

Before Pia could get another word out, Thor kissed her. He peeled off her drawers and chemise. When she was completely nude, he caressed her body, placing soft kisses along her breasts. Pia moaned when he brought one of her rosy nipples into his mouth, savoring its taste. The man sure knew how to kiss, and Pia wanted him to put his lips all over her body. Wherever his mouth touched, her body blazed with need and pleasure.

Thor drifted down and kissed the inside of her thighs. He spread her legs wide as his face drifted to her very core. He used his hands to open her wider, and one of his fingers gently stroked her. She moaned when his tongue darted out and found her sensitive spot. He licked and sucked until Pia thrashed wildly on the bed. She felt the culmination of something grow inside of her. As his mouth caressed her, his fingers stroked her, pumping in and out, until she screamed out in ecstasy.

The pleasure was so intense she didn't know how much more she could possibly take. He kept moving his fingers in and out of her, while his thumb caressed the sensitive nub. Every sensation made her burn, and her flesh heated, turning a rosy pink as moans of pure bliss escaped her mouth. She bucked against him, needing something more, but she didn't understand what her body craved. All she knew was something was missing.

Once again she saw stars as the world exploded around her. It was the most amazing feeling she had ever felt. It wasn't possible to feel this good. *What has Thor done to me?*

Before she finished the thought, Thor shifted her. He spread her legs wider and entered her slowly. He inched his way inside of her until he was fully seated within her quivering body. The pain caused her to bite her tongue and whimper. It hurt to take him inside of her. Everything had felt so good, and then he went and ruined it by pushing himself inside of her narrow passage.

"Shhh, it only hurts the first time, love. I promise the next time will be all pleasure."

He moved in and out of her, his pace steadily increasing. At first, she wanted to shove him off, but the more he moved, the better it felt. Pia's desire grew with each thrust. She wanted him deeper, harder, faster. She wrapped her legs around his waist, finding her own rhythm to match his movements. The sensations building up in her grew and Pia craved more. She couldn't get enough of him.

"Yes, like that, squeeze me, Pia. Good God, you feel so good. I can't hold out much longer. Come with me."

He kissed her again as he thrust deeper and faster. The movements brought Pia over the edge, and it was even better than the explosion she'd experienced earlier. This was a completion. It was just —right.

She screamed Thor's name as she came. He whispered her name as if it was a benediction. He soon followed and released himself inside her. He rolled to his side pulling her along with him. He curled his body around hers and held her as he fell asleep. Pia couldn't believe he was able to sleep after something so monumental, but she soon drifted off herself.

CHAPTER TEN

PIA WOKE UP IN SLOW DEGREES, AND THOR WAS STILL passed out next to her. She extricated herself from his embrace, getting out of the bunk as quietly as possible. She located her pantaloons and chemise lying on the floor where he had discarded them. Pia grabbed her dress and stepped into it, fastening the buttons as quickly and quietly as she could.

Now they were married, she hoped Thor would be more lenient in his desire to keep her confined in their cabin. Surely now he would start leaving the door unlocked. Pia was desperate to get off of the ship and go see her grandpere. She picked up her shoes and carried them out the door Thor had left unlocked. Thank the Lord. I can try to get away.

He must have felt secure in his ownership of her,

because he hadn't bothered to ensure she couldn't escape. Finally, the pirate was getting sloppy. He would soon discover she was capable of taking care of herself. He may have just given her the greatest pleasure she had ever known, but he also had used her in the worst possible way. She didn't want to consider what other complications might arise from what they had just done. Pia was well aware they could have created a baby, but she didn't have time to think about it. She needed to get away, and this may be her only opportunity.

When she was far enough away from the cabin that she felt safe, she put her shoes on. It was difficult, but she managed to be as silent as possible as she crept on deck. Pia walked on her toes across the creaking timbers, cringing every time a small squeak emitted from underneath her feet.

She looked up realizing they were still anchored in the harbor at Bordeaux. The docks were in the distance, but it shouldn't take her long to get to shore. She scanned the sides of the ship and spotted two of the crew climbing up a ladder. They vacated a dinghy to board the ship, and the bosun greeted them as they walked onto the deck.

Pia's heart beat heavily in her chest as she hid from their view. She was terrified they would

discover her hiding place. Standing as still as possible, she controlled her breathing so she wouldn't
make any unnecessary noise. Pia took the time to
still all of her movements, relaxing enough to listen
to their exchange.

"Is everything taken care of?" the bosun asked.

"Yes, sir. We dropped the priest back at his parish
and dumped the comte at his estate."

Estate? Grandpere had an estate in Bordeaux? Pia
had thought he lived in Calais.

"Very good. You may retire for the night and give
a full report to the captain in the morning. He is not
to be disturbed tonight. The captain changed his
mind, and we will set sail at dawn, please be
prepared to lift anchor."

There were no crew members anywhere else on
deck. The ship was almost like a ghost ship. That
couldn't be how it was normally. Where did all of the
crew go? Who was taking care of the ship? Pia had to
try to get to the dinghy and row to shore. Then she
could find her grandpere. Once she saw him, she
would have the chance to explain everything. He
would understand she really didn't have a choice.

As soon as the bosun was far enough away, Pia
scrambled to the ladder and climbed down into the
dinghy. She wasn't concerned for her own well-

being, but she was desperate to see how her grand-pere had fared. She may be the pirate's wife, but she could still make decisions for herself.

Her arms grew sore with each push of the oars through the water. Her strength was limited because of her small stature, but she managed to row herself to the nearest dock. Once the boat was next to the dock, Pia scrambled to the top and walked as fast as she could. Her breaths fell in pants from her mouth in the cold night air. She rubbed her hands together trying to warm them as she strolled across the docks.

The first thing she needed to do was find out where her grandpere's estate was. Pia didn't get very far before she was grabbed. She didn't even have time to scream before the unknown assailant dragged her away.

THOR WOKE UP AND STRETCHED. He had never felt so relaxed in his entire life. He wanted to experience those sensations all over again. Thor was blissfully happy at the results of loving his new bride. He rolled over to pull Pia to his side.

He sat up with a start. His cheeks heated with

anger. She wasn't in his bed. Where did the little minx go? She couldn't have gone far. Thor rolled off the bed and pulled on his clothing. He stormed up to the quarterdeck. Thor stomped his way to the cabin shared by his bosun and first mate and knocked on the door.

Thor waited for someone to come to the door. It opened to reveal his bosun, staring at him. "Corny, have you seen my wife?"

"No, Captain, I assumed she was with you."

"Well clearly she is not. Search the ship. Locate her at once." Thor watched as Corny woke the first mate.

The bosun and first mate rang the bell for all hands on deck. The crew searched everywhere, but Pia was nowhere to be found. It was only after several minutes of searching they realized the dinghy was gone. Pia had jumped ship.

Thor roared at them to get another dinghy ready. He was going to search for his wife and wring her little neck once he found her. She was his. How dare she leave him. He was blistering mad, his face heating with every word he shouted. Never before had he experienced a mixture of anger and fear. Thor required Pia be safely returned, but mostly he just needed her.

Pᴜᴀ ᴡᴀs sʜᴏᴠᴇᴅ into a carriage and quickly settled onto a seat. She didn't know who had grabbed her, but it couldn't be good. She slapped him. She was getting tired of people kidnapping her. Damn them all for thinking she was something they could throw around. What's wrong with people these days?

The man who had grabbed her rubbed his face to alleviate the sting. "Now, was that really necessary?"

Captain Devere sat across from her in the carriage. So, Thor hadn't killed him. She really did assume a lot about the man that was probably not true.

"Yes, you had no right to grab me and shove me in this carriage. I was frightened. It wasn't like I knew who was yanking me into this conveyance. It's a natural reaction for someone being kidnapped."

"I can assure you, I only have your best interests at heart," Captain Devere said.

Pia looked up at him. "Why did you take me?"

"I was asked to retrieve you by Comte Dubois. You made it a much easier task by rowing to shore. I must thank you for that. It made my job less dangerous."

"You are taking me to grandpere?"

"Yes, my dear, you may rest easy. You will be safe in his care in less than twenty minutes."

"When did you get here?" Pia asked. "I thought the pirate murdered everyone on board the ship. Is Tully alive? Thor had implied that he didn't kill anyone. Well he kind of told me that he hadn't killed everyone—but how was I to know if he was telling the truth or not. I'm relieved to see you are alive and well Captain."

"Yes, your maid is fine. She is at your grandpere's estate. He had her settled into the servants' quarters, and she will be there to assist you tomorrow."

Pia nodded her head. "Good. I know you mean well, Captain, but I don't know you. I want to look in on her myself as soon as possible."

Pia settled down on the seat, resting her head on the side of the carriage. One thing was certain. Her grandpere was alive. He wouldn't have been able to send someone to retrieve her if Thor had murdered him.

She needed to speak to her grandpere. There were a lot of questions she wanted to ask him. Pia hoped he was prepared to answer all of them, because she wanted the truth. Once she heard both sides of this sordid mess, she could decide the best course of action. She knew Thor would eventually come after her. Thor was tenacious and would not give up easily. Pia only hoped she had enough time to hear her grandpere's side before Thor caught up with her. She was grateful Thor hadn't murdered the ship's crew or Tully. It made it easier to accept her growing feelings for the wicked pirate.

CHAPTER ELEVEN

THOR NEEDED TO BEAT ON SOMETHING IN THE WORST way, so he swung around and punched the nearest wall as hard as he could. The pain he felt pulsing through his fist helped him focus on the real issue. His needed to retrieve his wife and forget about his increasing fury. His rage was so great that if any of his crew members had gotten near him they would have encountered serious bodily harm. Before he had boarded the dinghy, he had bellowed at his crew to get the ship prepared to leave port. When he returned with Pia, he fully intended to set sail immediately.

They had been too slow getting the dinghy ready, and as a result, he had missed Pia by mere minutes. Thor arrived at the dock just in time to see Pia being shoved into a nearby carriage. Captain Devere quickly jumped into the conveyance after her.

Thor found a hack as soon as he was able and demanded the driver go to the comte's nearby estate. It was the only place Devere could possibly be taking his wife.

The journey to Comte Dubois's estate would be brief, but it gave him time to reflect quietly on the situation. He should have realized Renny would try to take his granddaughter back. Thor had gotten sloppy, thinking he had won. Damn the comte for being such an evil bastard. So it looked like he would have to kill the comte after all. Thor was not leaving his wife in that man's care. Pia had become his everything in a very short time. He would not leave her in the vindictive hands of the comte. Thor wouldn't put it past him to harm his own grand-daughter if it suited his purposes.

Thor sat back, leaning his head against the side of the carriage combing his fingers through his disheveled hair. He wouldn't be able to live with himself if something bad happened to Pia. Thor tilted his head toward the sky praying he would get to the estate in time to get Pia out unharmed.

PIA ANXIOUSLY CLUTCHED her hands in her lap as their conveyance navigated the narrow road. The carriage rattled, shaking the seats as it traveled down the lane to her grandpere's estate. Captain Devere had assured her it shouldn't take more than twenty minutes for them to journey there. She sincerely hoped he was correct because the carriage was becoming increasingly more uncomfortable with each bump it rolled over.

Pia was growing weary of all the drama surrounding her life over the past couple of weeks. She should have been able to mourn her father in peace. Instead, she had been forced to leave her home and then kidnapped.

As they traveled, Devere told her what happened on the ship after Thor had taken her. Tully had been the only one Thor's crew hadn't tied up. When she wandered on deck and found the captain tied to the mast, she quickly freed him. The captain then went down and released his crew out from the cargo hold. They raised the sails and sailed toward France with due haste. There had been minimal damage done to the ship when Thor had attacked it. The damage inflicted had been meant to intimidate more than harm anyone aboard the ship.

Once they had arrived in port, they traveled to

the comte's estate. He had been too late to meet him before Thor's men had taken the comte aboard the Sea Rover. Once the comte was dropped off at his estate, he dispatched Captain Devere to retrieve her from Thor.

When they arrived at her grandpere's estate, the captain escorted her into the house. It was a beautiful manor at the end of a long driveway lined with large trees. As impressive as it was in the dark, it had to be breathtaking during the day.

Devere lead Pia into her grandpere's drawing room where she found him lounging in a chair nursing a glass of brandy. He jumped up as she marched into the room and hugged her tightly in his arms. Pia felt safe snuggled deep in her grandpere's burly arms. She heard Captain Devere shut the door as he left the room.

Comte Dubois took a step back and looked at Pia. "Thank the Lord they were able to save you from that demon's clutches."

"Grandpere, did you really try to kill him?"

"Don't be ridiculous, Pieretta. I never tried to kill him. He was like the son I never had, and his father was one of my dear friends."

"Then why does he think you tried to murder him?"

"It is a misunderstanding, I assure you. I loved the boy. I would not have killed him. It is sad what he has turned into. I cannot abide the life he has chosen to live. I was trying to save him, as I tried to explain on the ship. Perhaps, if I had gotten to him sooner—he is just not the same man I knew. He is dangerous, and you should not have married him. I'm sorry, my dear, but that was very reckless of you. We will have it annulled as soon as possible."

"That would be difficult to get, considering the marriage was consummated," Thor said with a drawl as he sauntered into the room.

Pia gasped. How did he get to Grandpere's estate so fast? She was sure he had been fast asleep when she left the ship. She assumed she would have more time to get answers. Why couldn't he have been a little slower in coming after me?

Comte Dubois took one look at Thor and then shouted for Captain Devere to come back into the drawing room.

"If you are looking for the captain, he is indisposed at the moment," Thor said as he made his way over to Pia.

"Damn you, Torrington. You cannot have my granddaughter."

Thor ignored the comte and continued walking

toward Pia.

"Why are you here, Thor?" Pia asked him.

"I thought that was clear, love. I missed my wife. I came to find her, because clearly she's lost. Wives are supposed to remain naked in bed next to their husbands awaiting another round of loving. We clearly have some miscommunication going on between us. You know where you belong, Pia. Get ready to leave now."

Pia looked at him with barely restrained belligerence. "No."

The shock and anger on Thor's face was palpable. His steely blue gaze was glued to her face as the lines of his mouth became tight from clenching his jaw. The muscles in his cheeks twitched, his face flushed with anger. He glared at Pia. "I must have heard you wrong, dear. You are my wife, and you will leave with me now. Did you forget our agreement?"

"No. I remember it quite clearly, and I want to make a new agreement."

"I must admit you have piqued my interest. What changes did you want to make, love?"

"I will not remain with a man that clearly does not love me and has no respect for my wishes. I want to be able to visit my family. My grandpere is all I have left."

Thor scoffed at her statement, his eyebrow raised with derision. His gaze locked with hers. "Your grandpere is a murderous villain, Pia. I will not tolerate you being in his presence. We will work through the rest of our issues once we take leave of this wretched place."

"Well that's too damn bad, because I will spend time with him."

"Enough," the comte shouted.

Pia and Thor turned to look at Comte Dubois. He was holding a pistol, and it was aimed at the both of them. Her grandpere had been lying to her. He had always meant for Thor to die. Her husband had been right for the pistol was clearly aimed at him.

"If the marriage can't be annulled, clearly Pieretta, dear, you need to be made a widow."

"But Grandpere you said you didn't try to kill him!"

"I lied. It's what I do. I couldn't afford for him to see that I was pocketing some of the funds from the company. I wasn't solvent and needed them to get by. The dowry I gave your mother was all I had left. It took me years to build my fortune back. I will not let this pirate take away everything I have built."

"You built it using my money, Renny. You had no right to help yourself to my funds. My life has been turned upside down by your greed, and I'll make sure you pay for that," Thor said.

Thor pushed Pia aside, diving for the gun. He struggled with Renny to gain control over the pistol, each trying to get a firm grasp on it. The two of them fell to the floor, rolling around. They wrestled for control of the pistol, trying to get it away from one another. As they struggled to gain control, the gun went off.

The sound of the gun echoed throughout the room. Everything started to move in slow motion. Pia's scream rattled the windows. Nothing was clear, and no one was moving quickly enough for her to know if either one of them had been hurt. With her heart pumping wildly in her chest, she ran over and fell beside the two motionless bodies. What should I do? Please let them be okay. Grandpere was a bad man, but she still didn't want him to die. Thor meant more to her than she wanted to admit.

A small movement caught her attention out of the corner of her eye, and she turned her head to see if it was real or not. Thor slowly turned over, and Pia immediately noticed a spot of blood near the top of his white shirt.

"Thor?" Pia asked hesitantly. Was he okay? In that moment, Pia realized how much he had come to mean to her. Without realizing it, the damned pirate had found a way into her heart.

"I'm okay, Pia. Your grandpere is bleeding all over me though. Send someone for a physician."

Pia ran out the door calling for a servant to come quickly. The butler arrived in response to her deafening screams for help. Pia grabbed his jacket, telling him to send for a physician. He pulled himself out of her grasp and retreated to find help.

Pia's attention immediately returned to her grandpere. She felt faint. The comte's face was as white as a ghost, and Pia scrambled over to his side. She had to do something to help him. She looked across the room. Thor stood in the corner watching her.

"Don't just stand there, go get me something to hold on his wound. He's bleeding all over the carpet. Help me please, Thor. I know he is your enemy, but he will always be my grandpere."

Thor nodded at her and pulled a handkerchief from his pocket, handing it to her.

"It won't help, Pia, but it is yours to use as you wish."

"Thank you, Thor, I appreciate your help. I have to do everything possible to help him."

Pia knelt next to her grandpere, placing the

handkerchief on the wound. His color wasn't improving. She turned his face in her hands and leaned over to see if he was still breathing. His breaths were shallow. Pia feared he wouldn't survive long enough for a physician to help, and tears welled in her eyes and rolled down her cheeks. She silently begged the Lord to save him.

As she wordlessly prayed, Tully ran into the room.

"Miss Pieretta, I heard you scream. Oh dear," Tully said, as her face grew pale at the sight of the comte bleeding all over her charge. "Is he dead?"

"Not yet, you fool. Don't just stand there, go in the hall and wait for the physician. Bring him in here immediately upon his arrival." Pia scolded her.

Tully ran out of the room. At least that was one less thing she had to worry about, she knew for sure Tully was well.

Pia watched as her grandpere opened his eyes. The pain glazed his expression. His voice broke with each word he tried speak, begging for her to understand.

"I'm sorry, Pia. Wanted what was best for you. I love you..." Those were the comte's final words as his last breath drifted away. Pia screamed in agony.

CHAPTER TWELVE

Life was full of decisions, and Pia had to make plenty in her lifetime. She knew there were certain things thrust upon a person in their lifetime which they had no control over. Love and death were prominent reminders of this. Pia's experience with love had been very limited. She knew one thing for certain: love could bring her joy or unimaginable sorrow, even if that love happened to be reciprocated. Death on the other hand had its own judgment and resolution. Her grandfather had paid for his actions with his life.

Pia prepared to bury her grandpere and say her final goodbye. Several important thoughts floated through her mind as the final preparations were made. Was Grandpere really gone forever? What was going to happen with Thor, now that he finally had his revenge? *How can I forgive him?* Does he even care about me?

With the help of Grandpere's solicitor, she was able to get through all of the funeral arrangements. Pia buried her grandpere at his estate in Bordeaux. It was a small service. The only people in attendance were a few of her grandpere's servants, Tully, Pia, and of course, her husband. Thor stayed by her side through it all, offering what little comfort she would allow.

All she saw when she looked at him was his chest covered in her grandpere's blood. She didn't know if she could stay with him. She still didn't believe he loved her. It was clear her feelings for him had changed during the time she had been his prisoner. She never believed she would ever fall in love.

When he kidnapped her, she had been so very afraid of what he would do to her, but, in the end, she had begun to trust him. At the very least she had come to believe he wouldn't truly harm her. It helped to see the evidence that he wasn't as dastardly as she'd believed. Tully alive and pestering her on a daily basis was enough of a reminder.

Pia was acquainted with all of Thor's faults and well aware he was capable of almost anything. After all, he did orchestrate her abduction. Pia knew she was a fool for letting herself fall in love with him. No matter how much she tried, she couldn't stop her foolish heart's devotion to him. How is it possible to fall in love so fast? She wanted him to return her love, and she desired him with an intense passion. But nothing would torture her more than staying in a loveless marriage. If he wasn't capable of caring for her, let alone loving her, she wouldn't stay with him. She needed more. If she couldn't have it, she would seek out someone to file for a divorce herself.

Still lost in her own thoughts, she didn't hear Thor walk into her grandpere's study. Pia had enclosed herself in the room, sitting on a comfortable divan to wallow in her misery. When she looked up and saw him standing so close, her heart skipped a beat.

He looked down at her with sympathy in the depths of his blue eyes. "Pia, the ship is ready to set sail whenever you're ready." His voice was interwoven with understanding.

With a petulant look firmly fixed on her face, she looked up at him. "I am not sailing away with you, Thor."

"Like hell you're not. You're my wife, and you belong with me."

"Do you honestly think I want to live like a pirate? What kind of life is that? What if we have children? Will they join the crew and plunder ships for bounty alongside you?"

"No. We will go back to England. I have responsibilities there that have neglected for far too long. I am a viscount, and I have an estate to reclaim. Your grandfather had me declared dead, so I will have to fight to regain my title. I don't want to be a pirate, Pia. Please come with me so we can build a life together."

Pia nodded. She could see he needed to do that. He did not need her with him to accomplish it. There was no give and take. He took it all and gave nothing in return. He said nothing about loving and needing her. Once again, he selfishly planned on using her to gain something he felt was his due. The sad thing was he didn't even need her to reclaim his title. He could go back and live his life without ever seeing her again if he wished.

"You do not need me, Thor. You don't require me for anything. You should go back and claim your title. While you are there, file for divorce. I don't care on what grounds. We are better off without each other."

"No," Thor said with belligerence in his voice. "I

will never be better off without you. How could I be? Please, Pia, don't fight me on this. You are my wife, and I want you to board the Sea Rover with me today."

"I'm not going to fight with you, Thor. I am not going with you, and I will not remain with a man who doesn't love and respect me."

"Who the hell told you I don't love or respect you?"

"Well you haven't exactly told me that you do. You fail to take my desires into consideration. You dictate to me and never ask if I am okay with your orders. I am not going to live with someone who is going to take me for granted. No, I would rather die. Because you no longer have anything to hold over me, that is the only option left."

Pia turned her back to him, deciding the conversation was over. She leaned her head against the back of the couch and closed her eyes. She assumed he had left because he ceased speaking. Pia's eyelids fluttered open, and she saw Thor's blue eyes staring directly into hers.

Thor cleared his throat and spoke, his voice shaking, overflowing with emotion. "Pia, I have loved you from the moment I saw you. I never intended to actually marry you. My original plan involved pretending to do it and then using you, but meeting you changed everything. No one ever plans to find love, and I certainly never planned on finding it with you. The thought of you leaving scares me more than anything. I cannot imagine a life without your fire to warm me each night. From the instant I met you, I planned on keeping you. I know I've blundered with everything I've done. Not respecting your wishes was only to protect you. Your grandpere was an evil man, and you didn't see it. With every part of my soul, I swear I never meant to make you feel less than you are. I could never hurt you."

Pia stared at him. She waited, wondering if she should believe him. There was nothing she wanted more than to believe what he was telling her.

His voice had faltered and became husky with emotion. Thor's expression showed remorse. His gaze implored hers as if pleading with her.

"If you don't love me, I will understand," he said. "Being without you could never make me happy, but I will let you go if that's what you truly want. I would rather take my dagger and push it through my own heart then ever knowingly hurt you again."

Pia stared at him in shock. She never expected that he would actually return her feelings. She looked down at her arm and pinched herself to make sure it wasn't a dream. Ouch, nope this is real. Thor always had a way of stealing her breath, surprising her at every turn. Her lips curled up into a sumptuous smile as happiness overtook her soul. Her heart pounded with excitement when she finally accepted his words.

It was imperative she heard him say it one more time to make sure she'd heard him right. "You really love me?"

"Yes, I love you. Do you love me, even a little? Can you stay with me? Please come back to England with me. I need my viscountess to help me reestablish my holdings, and I need her to hold each night. I want her to be the mother of my children. Without you, my life wouldn't be worth living. Please, Pia, come home with me."

"Yes. Yes, Thor, I love you too. I will come home with you. There isn't any place on this Earth I would rather be." She stood and rushed over to him, throwing herself into his arms.

Thor gathered her tightly against his chest wrapping his arms around her as he hugged her close. Pia tilted her face up and met his eyes as his lips pressed down on hers. Thor plundered her in all the ways she loved most, and Pia enjoyed every minute of the passion they shared.

EPILOGUE

IN THE PAST, THOR HAD MANY DEMONS HIDING INSIDE of his soul, and they soured certain aspects of his life. He had something miraculous happen to him that allowed him to exorcise those dark areas. An angel of mercy had taken pity on his possessed black core and helped to bring him back to the light. In those moments, his life changed as his heart started to feel again and the darkness bled from its depths.

When Thor found Pia, his soul was cleansed. She was the angel who showed him how love could change his life. His existence was forever altered when he fell in love with the spirited beauty. If someone had asked him before he met Pia if he believed in love, he would have laughed at their audacity. Love? No that was for fools. *Well color me a fool because I am blissfully in love with my wife, and I wouldn't change it for anyone.*

If he had never kidnapped her to get revenge on her grandpere, his soul would still be a dark carcass of unhappiness. Thor needed her light to balance the dark shadows that overtook his spirit. They were opposites, put on Earth to balance each other out. To have her love him as much as he loved her was a blessing he didn't feel he deserved. He would never make the mistake of hurting her again. He had made a promise he would never break. Pia was everything to him.

Sitting in his study on his main English estate, Thor was lost in thought, reminiscing about the day he met the love of his life. She wasn't perfect. Everyone had flaws. He loved every one of her imperfections, because to him, she was beyond perfection. She was more priceless than the most expensive jewel. Her flaws were what made her unique. Pia was irreplaceable. She was his flawed jewel.

Thor rested his chin in his hands as a contented half smile tugged at his lips. He had a good life with Pia and their two children. It wasn't long after they returned to England, they got the happy news that Pia was expecting their first child.

As with everything in their lives, it shouldn't have been a surprise that even their children refused to do things the easy way. Almost exactly nine months after their wedding, Pia gave birth to twins, a girl and a boy. Lilliana Rose was born five minutes before her brother, Liam Robert. Lily had dark hair and cobalt blue eyes similar to her father, where Liam favored his mother with pale blond hair and light blue eyes.

Nothing could make him happier than to spend the rest of his life watching his children grow. Thor wanted all of the experiences fatherhood had to offer. As long as he had Pia and the twins by his side, his happiness was assured.

Thor turned as a little girl with black curls toddled into the room. A short time later, she was followed by a petite blonde woman carrying a small boy in her arms.

Pia looked over at Thor, her face flushed red from chasing their bundles of joy. "It's your turn. They want daddy to tell them their favorite story. You know the one."

Thor knew exactly which story they wanted to hear. It was the best fairy tale in all creation. It was the story of a flawed jewel and her dastardly pirate.

They wanted to hear about adventure, love, and how their parents found each other.

Thor sat on the sofa and beckoned them close. "I'm happy to tell it. Please, come sit down by daddy, Lily, Liam."

The three-year-old twins crawled up onto his lap and waited for him to begin. Pia took a seat on the corner of the sofa her gaze softening as he looked into his eyes.

He settled them against him and began his story.

"Once upon a time, a pirate set out on the high seas..."

EXCERPT: A TREASURED LILY

A MARSDEN ROMANCE BOOK TWO

DAWN BROWER

CHAPTER 1

"I JUST DON'T THINK IT'S A GOOD IDEA."

"Nonsense." Lilliana Marsden looked up at her best friend, Lady Gemma Kemsley, and frowned. "It's a brilliant idea. My father is being unreasonable about allowing me to travel to America. The plantation in South Carolina is my inheritance. It's about time I claimed it."

"It's not going to work for you to just show up and claim it though. I don't get why you are in such a hurry. You know full well you won't inherit it until you marry." Gemma reached up and smoothed over her sanguine curls, tucking a loose strand behind her ear.

"Well, that's not entirely true." Lilliana's lips twitched into a cheeky smile; it helped to have a little insight into how her parents worked. Gemma didn't know how much she'd gotten away with over the years. Eavesdropping had become a habit of hers. A person could find out the most interesting things quite by accident. When she overheard her parent's most recent conversation she couldn't help the glee that filled her soul. Reining in her excitement had taken an enormous amount of restraint. She needed to leave England and start the life she envisioned for herself. One she had complete control over. Her parent's still hoped she would settle down and get married, but they didn't know her true reasons. "I stumbled across a bit of information that may help me to achieve my goal."

"I don't understand. Did you find a way to inherit it early?"

Lilliana got up, walked to the window of the sitting room, and pulled open the curtains. She stared out at the garden and pondered how to explain what she overheard, and exactly how it fit into her idea to get everything she wanted. Various shades of roses, red, orange, and white, scattered across the garden in a pattern that reminded Lilliana of a kaleidoscope. The garden remained one of the places that she turned to when she needed to reflect on what floated through her mind. It calmed her and made it possible for her to think rationally about any issue that arose in her life. Something about being surrounded by the plant life helped her to think and form her plans with a clear head. Lilliana needed to get Gemma to aid her in her quest to leave England. They worked their magic on her as she calmly let the curtain go and turned back towards her best friend.

"I don't *ever* plan on getting married. I told you that the day we met. My parents still insisted on a season or two. They believe everyone is capable of finding love. They don't understand they are a rarity."

A sting of pain stabbed through her heart, Lilliana rubbed her chest in an attempt to erase the phantom ache. After her disastrous first season, she knew quite well how unusual it was for a love match to exist within the ton. Her choices were lecherous old men and scheming vermin only after her money. There was one man though who made her want to believe he really loved her. She found out the hard way he only wanted to use her. She was thankful he didn't achieve his goal and Lilliana came out relatively unscathed, but the damage to her belief in love sat firmly in place.

"Most matches are made for business or political

reasons. It's all about money and there is no way I'm handing over mine to a male to control."

Gemma tilted her head and crinkled her nose in confusion. Lilliana knew she didn't get it. Her friend wanted to get married and have children. The two years difference in their ages showed when they discussed the possibility of matrimony. In time, Lilliana believed Gemma would look back on this conversation with clarity. In the midst of starting her first season and barely seventeen years old, Gemma still approached life with rose-colored glasses on. For a brief moment in time Lilliana had worn that same veil of hope; her parent's love inspired her enough to want to find it herself.

Reality came crashing in like a bolt of lightning and shattered every ounce of optimism she held within her. Lilliana realized finding love at the various parties hosted within London society equaled finding a mythical creature. The chances of finding a unicorn would be an easier feat. So she gave up on love and formed a new plan for her life.

"I still think you are being preposterous. Why are you so against marriage?" Gemma folded her arms across her chest and stared at Lilliana. Her eyes pinning her in place as she spoke. "That's what a lady is expected to do after all. I just don't understand how you plan on claiming your inheritance without the benefit of a husband to help you get it."

Lilliana could feel her lips twitch into a smile. Her mother often commented on how Lilliana received all her father's traits, even his less than desirable ones. William Thorston Marsden, fifth Viscount Torrington, had a way of getting what he wanted out of people. She admired that character-istic in her father and sought to emulate it. Still, she wished she had been lucky enough to get her moth-er's pale blonde hair instead of her father's dark curls. In Lilliana's mind, her twin brother, Liam, was blessed because he inherited her mother's coloring.

"I suppose I should explain it so you won't be left in the dark. I'll need your assistance after all."

Gemma got up from her seat and crossed to the window where Lilliana still stood. "You're my best friend. I'll help if I can, but I'm going to be honest and say I don't like this. I don't want to lose you. Please reconsider."

"I will miss you, but I need to find my own way. Please understand this is the best thing for me."

Gemma sighed and then pulled Lilliana into her arms for a hug. Lilliana wrapped her arms around her best friend. She had been curious about Gemma once she realized who she was. Lady Gemma

Kemsley had been the girl her father wanted her brother to marry when they were younger. She sought out an introduction to get her measure and hadn't been disappointed in the young woman. They had only been friends for a few months, but in all her nineteen years she had never been close to another female her age. It didn't matter that a couple years separated their age; they were a different kind of soul mate. They appreciated each other on a level that no one else ever could or would.

"I'll try to understand. I really will, but I'm never going to like it. You are my only friend. I will always wish for you to be near me..." Gemma pulled away from Lilliana and clasped their hands together. "Tell me what I can do to help."

Lilliana knew she could count on Gemma. Elation filled her as she could envision how it would all work out. Now all she needed to do was give her all the details so she could do her part in the plan.

"I overheard my parents talking. I had no intention of listening until I heard my name spoken. I found out some interesting things that I never knew. Not the least being that Mama never intended to get married and Father had blackmailed her into agreeing to be his wife."

Gemma gasped. "What?"

"Makes you stop and question the validity of their love and all that doesn't it?"

Gemma's mouth hung open with shock radiating from her eyes. After a small pause while the information sank in she asked, "Why would he do such a thing?"

"Once upon a time Papa sailed his ship, the *Sea Rover*, as its pirate captain. Apparently he had a little feud with Mama's grandpere and she became the leverage he needed to enact his revenge. They came out of it okay, clearly as they are still together." Lilliana flipped her hand dismissively as she spoke. "The point is that Mama said that by the time I'm twenty if I still don't wish to wed, she planned on giving me the deed to the plantation in South Carolina."

Lilliana tried over and over to explain to her parents how much marriage was distasteful to her, without going into too much detail. If her father knew exactly how her heart had been bruised, he would have murderous intentions. The real issue was she didn't want anyone to know how naïve she had been. Now, she knew she could get what she wanted and nothing made her happier. Anxiety filled with equal swirls of excitement tumbled through her belly.

"That's still too long for me to wait. I won't be twenty until December and that is nine months away. What I want to do is sail there now and use my family position to gain control. My plans are not going to change just because nine months pass by."

"What good will that do? Without the deed securely in your control will they allow you to oversee the plantation? Isn't someone already there taking care of the property?" Gemma asked.

"There is an overseer yes. I'm hoping to convince him that the letter giving him orders to give me control got lost on the mail packet before my arrival. Come let's sit down in comfort as we work out the details." Lilliana grabbed Gemma's hand and led her to the settee. After they were seated she poured them both tea and handed a cup to her friend. Lilliana took a sip of tea before continuing their conversation. "I've thought a lot about what needs to be done. Even if the overseer doesn't believe I have control of the plantation no one has the authority to throw me off the property because it is owned by my family. If I have to wait, I'd rather do it in South Carolina."

Gemma nodded. "Okay, I suppose that makes sense. What do you need me to do?"

"Well the tricky part is leaving without letting my

parents know. First, I need to find a ship sailing to America. Once I book passage I'm going to need a way to get my trunks on board without raising suspicion. I'm not worried about funds. I've been saving all my pin money for months now." Lilliana gave Gemma a smile. Surely she would see how she thought of every possible issue in her plan.

"So how do you plan on getting your trunks on board the ship?"

"That is where you come in. Once I know what ship I'm on, I'd like you to invite me to come stay with you in the country for a week." Lilliana set her teacup down and gave Gemma her full attention. She really needed Gemma to help her. If she didn't, her whole plan would fall apart. Her eyes pleaded with Gemma as she spoke, "My family won't question it because they know that our schedule is relaxed at the moment. It will give me a reason to pack a trunk or two and have them loaded onto a carriage. The carriage with your family crest on it that is."

"Oh, I understand. You will have the carriage drop you off at the docks and our servants will unload your trunks to be delivered to the ship. They won't have a reason to let your family know that you're boarding the ship. The servants will assume they already know." Gemma nodded her head in understanding.

"I knew you'd get it." Excitement filled Lilliana's voice. "It's all coming together now. I only have one little facet to figure out before I can iron out the rest of the details. The first item I need to cross off my list is to figure out what ships are heading to America and if they are accepting passengers."

"However are you going to figure that out?"

"Oh, that's the easy part. I will just ask Liam," Lilliana proclaimed.

Gemma blinked several times before she asked, "Won't he find that suspicious?"

"Not at all," Lilliana said waving her hand. "He's constantly talking about the Marsden shipping line and its competitors. He just started to take over the business. Our father believes it's time for him to learn about his future inheritance."

"I see. When do you plan on getting the information out of him?"

"Tonight at the Silverton's ball. Father is making him escort me. I will make sure to have a friendly conversation with him in the carriage on our way."

"You have thought of everything. I'm sure it will work just the way you want it." A small smile grew on Gemma's face as she looked at Lilliana. "I just wish your plans didn't have to take you so far away from England. Why couldn't you have fallen in love with a nice earl or baron...or even a mere mister? Anything that might inspire you to stay where I have an actual possibility to visit you, chances are I'll never be able to travel to America to visit. Promise me you'll come back to see me."

"I promise to come back to see you. In the meantime, we'll keep in touch with lots and lots of letters. I want to know everything about your life and when you find the man of your dreams."

"Good. I suppose I should go. I'll see you tonight at the ball."

Gemma stood up and grabbed her pelisse. After she donned it, she walked over and gave Lilliana a quick hug. She watched as Gemma left the room and got up to walk back to the window to look at the rose garden. All she could do at this point was hope all of her plans went off without a hitch. Doubts clouded her mind as she knew from experience nothing ever went exactly as planned, and naught could be done to alleviate her anxiety. Lilliana decided to try and let it go. She turned and left the sitting room to find some kind of diversion. Perhaps a book would work to distract her thoughts away from any possible problems—thinking, or over thinking in her case, had always been her worst enemy. With a smile on her lips Lilliana strolled to the library. Dark feelings would not sink through and ruin her good mood. Preparation was the key to success. No one planned and schemed better than Lilliana Marsden.

ABOUT THE AUTHOR

USA TODAY Bestselling author, DAWN BROWER writes both historical and contemporary romance. There are always stories inside her head; she just never thought she could make them come to life. That creativity has finally found an outlet.

Growing up she was the only girl out of six children. She raised two boys into productive young men. There is never a dull moment in her life. Reading books is her favorite hobby and she loves all genres.

She is active on Facebook, Twitter, and Instagram. To follow her or can find more about her check out her website for the pertinent information:

www.authordawnbrower.com

bookbub.com/authors/dawn-brower

facebook.com/1DawnBrower

twitter.com/1DawnBrower

instagram.com/1DawnBrower

goodreads.com/dawnbrower

If It's Love (Amanda Mariel)

Odds of Love (Dawn Brower)

Believe In Love (Amanda Mariel)

Chance of Love (Dawn Brower)

Love and Holly (Amanda Mariel)

Love and Mistletoe (Dawn Brower

Bluestockings Defying Rogues

When An Earl Turns Wicked

A Lady Hoyden's Secret

One Wicked Kiss

Earl In Trouble

All the Ladies Love Coventry

One Less Scandalous Earl

Confessions of a Hellion

Coming Soon

The Vixen in Red

Marsden Descendants

Rebellious Angel

Tempting An American Princess

How to Kiss a Debutante

Loving an America Spy

Marsden Romances

A Flawed Jewel

A Crystal Angel

A Treasured Lily

A Sanguine Gem

A Hidden Ruby

A Discarded Pearl

Novak Springs

Cowgirl Fever

Dirty Proof

Unbridled Pursuit

Sensual Games

Christmas Temptation

Linked Across Time

Saved by My Blackguard

Searching for My Rogue

Seduction of My Rake

Surrendering to My Spy

Spellbound by My Charmer

Stolen by My Knave

Separated from My Love

Scheming with My Duke

Secluded with My Hellion

Coming Soon

Secrets of My Beloved

Spying on My Scoundrel

Shocked by My Vixen

Heart's Intent

One Heart to Give

Unveiled Hearts

Heart of the Moment

Kiss My Heart Goodbye

Heart in Waiting

Broken Curses

The Enchanted Princess

The Bespelled Knight

The Magical Hunt

Ever Beloved

Forever My Earl

Always My Viscount

Infinitely My Marquess

EternallyMyDuke

Kismet Bay

Once Upon a Christmas

New Year Revelation

All Things Valentine

Luck At First Sight

Endless Summer Days

A Witch's Charm

All Out of Gratitude

Christmas Ever After

AFTERWORD

Thank you so much for taking the time to read my
book.
Your opinion matters!
Please take a moment to review this book on your
favorite review site and share your opinion with
fellow readers.

www.authordawnbrower.com

www.ingramcontent.com/pod-product-compliance
Lightning Source LLC
Chambersburg PA
CBHW032141170626
46808CB00006B/2326